Limitation

of

Life

Dedication

This book is dedicated to my two beautiful kids (Nia and Deuce). I hope that you understand that life is to be enjoyed while still trying to be the best person you can be. Success without happiness is meaningless. Even in your mistakes, be strong and carry on. Embrace life and be the leader and hero in it. Set goals and let no one tell you they are impossible to achieve until you attempt them yourself. Forever remember, my love for you is endless and every move in life I've made has been to better your life now and beyond. Take care and love, Daddy.

Limitation

of

Life

By

d. E. Rogers

Chapter One

Year 2025

With a noose tightly around her neck, the beautiful, caramel-skinned woman did everything possible to not end up being hung from the ceiling chandelier. At this moment, the only thing preventing that from occurring was her feet—and she was on her tippy toes—and the patience of the person sitting at the desk in front of her. Masked to conceal their identity and wearing white plastic gloves to prevent fingerprints from being left behind, the assailant furiously scribbled a note. It read:

> To my family and friends,
>
> I apologize for being so weak. I wish things could have gone better, but I don't see any other way out. I've tried for many years to fight these demons within me, but I can't do it anymore. I loved someone I shouldn't have ever loved, and it cost me dearly. I put my trust in Brodie, and he made me do things I will always regret. Please know that I love you all and will miss you. Bye for now.
>
> Love, Cymone

The gloved person turned around; the black ski-mask was snug on their head and face. The woman's, Cymone's, eyes filled with tears as she nervously focused on staying on her tippy toes and, at the same time, trying to make sure she could still breathe. For

Cymone, life meant everything, and it was slowly slipping away from her. She didn't want to die, especially in this manner.

"You're not getting away with this, Derek. I know that's you! Be a man and speak up, you sicko!" she cried out. "You're a coward who blames others for your crimes. You'll never be better than Brodie."

The person abruptly stood and rushed to her. It was obvious that the mention of Brodie had riled them up. The masked assailant slowly began to move the chair away from Cymone's feet. She struggled to stay balanced as she came closer to losing her footing. With her hands tied behind her back, there was nothing for her to grab on. Her eyes bulged out as she realized she couldn't escape and that her screams and begging meant nothing to anyone. She braced herself for the chair being snatched from under her feet. Her body became as tense as a stone, fearing the end was imminent.

As her feet neared the end of the chair seat, she let out one final scream. "I'm sorry. I never meant to hurt you. Please don't do this," she begged.

The masked person, without any hesitation, pulled the chair away. She began struggling to stop from choking as the person stared at her with a glimmer in their eyes of pure happiness. The masked person pulled off their mask revealing their identity to Cymone. By the widening of Cymone's eyes it was obvious that it wasn't the person she had assumed it was. As Cymone took her last breaths the hotel room door opened.

***

In the Wynn hotel on the Las Vegas Strip, Brodie Carmichael's bald head hung over the toilet as he vomited his guts out in one of the restrooms on the casino level floor. Even in his ill state, one could see Brodie's handsome looks and great physique. Though right now, he looked very pale for a black man. He clutched his stomach as he stared into the bowl at what he had recently eaten. A quick glance down and he saw his all-white shirt and pants were now covered in his vomit. His eyes rolled around in his head as he tried not to vomit anymore.

"I think they are trying to poison me. I got to call Cymone. We have to end this before someone dies," he said as his head fell off the toilet and hit the floor. Brodie looked up at the ceiling and then passed out on the floor. While laying out his phone rang and rang. The caller ID showed the name 'Sheila'.

On the other end, Sheila had a concerned look on her face as the call went to voicemail. "Brodie, pick up. I think the time machine has been compromised. You and Cymone need to be careful. Something isn't right. Call me immediately. I called Vegas PD and they are going to your room now to check on you."

Sheila hung up the phone. "We have to go back to the beginning to fix this. I don't understand what could have happened."

Year 2015

In his dorm room at Central State University in Wilberforce, Ohio, Brodie was lying down watching the NCAA March Madness basketball tournament Thursday night games. Feeling restless and tired, he took some pills to help him sleep. The bottle label read that it was Sheila's sample. About an hour later, when he started to slowly drift to sleep, someone knocked on his door. At first, he wasn't going to answer it. He figured it was one of his boys wanting him to go out drinking. Not in the drinking mood, he hoped his friend would just go away tonight. But the knocking persisted until it became annoying. He finally went to the door and opened it, and he was surprised to see that it was Trevor, the dorm's floor manager.

"Trevor, what's up?" Brodie asked with a surprised look on his face.

"Is your phone working?" Trevor looked over and saw his room phone was off the hook. "Your mother said it was an emergency," Trevor said, thinking in the back of his mind that someone important in Brodie's family must have died. "She's on the hallway phone."

"My mother?" Brodie said, trying to figure out why she would be calling this late. One of his biggest pet peeves was being surprised, and from the lateness of the call, he anticipated it wasn't good.

"Yeah, man, I wouldn't have beat down your door if she didn't say it was important."

Brodie slowly made his way over to the phone. He looked back at Trevor before putting the receiver next to his ear.

"Hey, Momma," he said softly.

His mother, Gloria Carmichael, was almost fifty years old. She'd had a hard life of struggle in the seventies and eighties, but she still tried as hard as she could to keep her family together and tight. She wanted to be strong for her son, but she couldn't. Family was vital to her, and losing anyone cut deep into her soul, but this time, the cut seemed even deeper.

She tried to speak, but her crying drowned out any words she had for him. All Brodie could hear in the midst of her frantic crying was Sheila's name.

"Momma, did something happen to Sheila?

Gloria took a deep breath. "Sheila is on life support," she mumbled.

"What does that mean?" Brodie asked as tears raced down his face. She was his big sister and best friend. "I just talked to her yesterday."

"They say she's probably not going to make it," his mother said, stuttering to get the words out.

"Who is they?" he asked feeling like the moment was too surreal that Sheila was about to die.

"The doctors, Brodie. They want me to pull the plug. They are saying it's nothing else they can do for her."

"Nooo…" Brodie slid to the floor, crying in the dorm's hallway. He clutched his chest as if having a heart attack.

"I don't want to do it, but she's brain dead. Only her heart is keeping her alive. There's nothing I can do to save my baby."

"What happened?" Brodie asked. "We were talking about school and work just yesterday. Now this?"

"Just come home. I love you, Brodie."

"What happened?" Brodie asked again. "I don't understand this."

Again, Gloria ignored the question. "I'll see you at home."

"Momma, maybe there's a chance for a miracle. Give it time. Please," Brodie begged as his fist hit the cement floor over and over again. The other students in the dorm felt for him as they tried to give him his grieving space.

"I'm sorry, baby. I can't have my baby be a vegetable for the rest of her life. I got to go. Bye."

"Okay, Momma, bye." Brodie let the phone go, but he stayed on the floor, crying.

After a few minutes, Trevor and some other guys came over, and they helped Brodie up and guided him to his room.

***

The next afternoon, Brodie made it home. When he arrived at the door of his family home, there were reporters and police officers everywhere. He made it through the circus of people to finally reach his mother, who was sitting on the couch staring at the TV set, which was turned off. He immediately gave her a hug and a kiss on the cheek. They sat there, speechless, for about a minute, holding hands and thinking about Sheila. With all the news and authorities at their home, Brodie knew there was more to his sister's death than his mother had led him to believe.

"Momma, what's going on?" he asked as he faced her.

Gloria was silent as she continued to stare off into space. It wasn't until he touched her hand that she really noticed him.

"Brodie, when did you get here?" she asked like he had just appeared out of thin air. "I'm so glad to see you." She gave him a hug and a kiss on the cheek.

"What's going on?" he asked.

"I didn't want to say anything over the phone, but your sister was murdered down the street coming back from the corner store. Someone walked up to her and shot her in the head."

"She was murdered? Why didn't you say that over the phone?" Brodie was numb as he processed the information.

"I'm still not understanding any of this myself," Gloria said, maintaining a steady voice even though her chin quivered. She didn't want Brodie to see how broken she was or for him to start worrying her mental state.

"Why are the police here? Shouldn't they be out looking for the people who murdered her?"

"They think she had something to do with this! Talking about this is an ongoing investigation. Sheila ain't did nothing to nobody." Gloria scowled at the sight of the officers ravaging through her home. "She was smart. Had a great job down there at the genetics lab. She volunteered at the school."

"I'm getting these people out of here." Brodie noticed that one of the police officers wore a suit and tie and approached him. "Excuse me, sir. Are you one of the people in charge here?"

The white man in the suit turned around and faced him. "Where were you at yesterday afternoon between 6 and 7 p.m.?" he asked in a thick country accent.

Brodie slit his eyes at the police officer. "Are you serious?"

"Everyone's a suspect until I clear them."

Brodie shook his head. "You people are ridiculous. Why are you in my mother's house? Don't you think she's been through enough? The killer isn't here. You policemen are morons thinking the person who killed my sister is in this house."

The officer grabbed Brodie and threw him up against the wall. He wanted to punch Brodie in the face, but saw the other officers staring over at them. "I'm taking you downtown, boy. You think you're real smart? I'll give you an education in law enforcement downtown at the precinct," the officer said in a low whispering southern accent.

Gloria rushed over to the officer and Brodie. "Let my son go! He just got here from college. He hasn't been home since Christmas. Get your hands off of him now!" she screamed, gaining the attention of everyone around them. An officer behind Gloria grabbed his gun and waited on her next move.

The officer who had grabbed Brodie quickly let him go.

"When are you all leaving?" Gloria asked with anger in her voice. "My daughter was no criminal."

"Then why was she fired last week from the lab? Her boss said she was terminated for stealing property."

"Sheila never stole anything in her life. It's time for you to leave," Gloria insisted.

The officer looked around at the other policemen searching the house for evidence. "We're almost done."

"Make it quick. I need to plan my daughter's funeral and don't want any of you here when I start."

Brodie saw the rage in his mother's eyes as the veins in her neck bulged out. He pulled her away, and they returned to the couch.

"Where is Daddy at?" he asked with a grimace.

His mother was slow to respond. "He went to work this morning."

Brodie rolled his eyes. "You got to be kidding me. What kind of man goes to work after his daughter dies? He's heartless."

"Brodie, you got to understand people grieve differently. He cares about Sheila."

"Like he cares for me and DeAndre?" Brodie smirked. "That man only cares for himself."

"He put a roof over your head and kept you fed."

"Yeah, but emotionally, he couldn't care less about any of us. Anyway, where are our family and friends?"

"You know black people. When they see the police searching your house, they don't want to get caught up in that mess. Sheila was so quiet that some of them actually thought that she was involved in something illegal."

"Did Sheila get fired last week for real?" Brodie asked, wondering if the police were just lying.

"Supposedly, yes. I talked to one of her co-workers, and they said that they don't think Sheila took anything. I think her boss is full of shit."

"What did she supposedly take?"

"Nobody knows," Gloria waved her hand dismissively. "All I know is that Sheila didn't do it."

"Did a KJ come by?"

"Who is that?" Gloria asked.

"Sheila mentioned KJ a couple of times the last couple of times we talked. She didn't mention it to you? You two talked about everything."

"Definitely didn't talk about a KJ."

Two police officers approached them. "We're all done here."

Brodie looked both officers in the eyes. "Are you going to catch the person who murdered my sister?"

"That's what our goal is."

Brodie smirked. "You know, coming in, I didn't see any police cars or officers at the corner store or even over there in that area. You guys aren't going to do any real work on finding her killer, huh?"

"You have to believe in the process," one of the officers replied.

"No offense, but your process stinks and leaves a lot of murders unsolved."

"Sorry you feel that way. Here's my card. If you remember anything that might help the case, please reach out to me."

Brodie's lip curled. "So, you want us to do your work?"

The officer stared Brodie down. "It takes a village. Isn't that what your people say?"

Brodie rolled his eyes. "Did you guys recover a weapon on the scene?"

"Yeah, we're testing it for prints now."

"So, what was the purpose of looking here if you got the weapon already?"

The officer rolled his eyes in annoyance. "Like I said, if you remember anything, please reach out. We do want to solve this crime. And I'm sorry for you and your mother's loss." He turned and walked out, and the other officers followed behind.

Once the final officer had left the house, Brodie got up and closed the door behind them. He looked outside as their cars drove off.

"Who would do this to my Sheila?" his mother cried out, letting her guard down now that they were alone. "I want the person who killed her dead."

Brodie went over and held his mother as they cried together.

"Man, I wish I knew who did this to Sheila. I swear I will kill them if I ever find them."

Gloria wanted the person dead, but she didn't want Brodie to do it. "I don't need you doing something stupid. I need you alive and not locked up."

"It just hurts. I want somebody to pay for this." He broke away from her. "I owe justice to Sheila."

"I know, baby, but we'll make it through this. We just have to lean on each other and be strong."

Brodie wasn't listening at all to his mother. He was fully consumed by thinking about finding and killing the person who had killed his sister.

Gloria saw that he was not listening to her. Brodie had always been a hardheaded child growing up. Once he made up his mind to do something, nothing could stop him. But him not listening didn't bother her that much; she wanted to talk about anything else besides Sheila's death. "So, what are your plans for school next year?"

Brodie paused for a moment. "I'm transferring to Purdue next fall. I have two years left and figure it would be best to be closer to home."

"Why not Notre Dame? It's even closer." Gloria smiled.

"Purdue is close enough for you to reach me and for me to come home to check on things. Plus, I never heard back from Notre Dame about being accepted or not."

His mother got up in her son's face and looked into his eyes. "You don't have to do this for me."

"No, I don't, but I'm doing this for our family."

Gloria placed her hand on Brodie's shoulder. "I do like the fact that you will be closer."

"When is DeAndre coming in?"

"Tonight. You know the military and their paperwork just to attend a funeral."

16

"It will be good to see him."

Gloria's face lit up. "My two boys back together."

"Maybe DeAndre can help me find the killer."

"You know your brother has a bad temper. Don't get him started."

"Okay, I won't, but I'm still going to look on my own. Something isn't right about this."

Gloria stared at him. "Brodie, leave that alone. Whoever did this is dangerous. I can't lose two kids. That, I can't handle. Promise me."

"I can't let her killer run free," Brodie said, shaking his head.

"Promise me you'll let this go. Killing only leads to more killing. You want to be dead or in prison?"

"I'm too smart for that."

"That's what everyone says a few moments before dying or getting arrested."

Brodie knew this was an argument he couldn't win, so he gave up to pacify his mother for now. "Okay, you win."

"Good. Just go to Purdue and be a student. One day, you'll be the top physicist in the world. I love you."

Brodie hugged her. "I love you, too."

His mother studied the sadness on his face. "You know you can take a break from school for a year. Dealing with death isn't easy."

"I know, but I think I can handle it."

Chapter Two

Brodie's first school year at Purdue went by in a blur. He spent the entire time consumed with trying to find out who might have killed his sister. He called the South Bend Police Department almost every other day, asking for updates on who might have gunned her down. The police provided nothing substantial, which led him to believe they had given up on the case, and he quickly lost faith in the police ever finding the killer. During this time, his education suffered greatly since he missed a majority of his classes and flunked most of them as well. At the Christmas break, he received the customary letter from the Dean putting him on academic probation and notifying him that if his grades didn't improve, he would be expelled at the end of the year. The next semester didn't mean anything to him either, and he anticipated getting the boot from school since he made no real effort to do his schoolwork. He went to class and went through the motions, but he never studied for tests or completed his assignments. A naturally smart kid, he was able to do satisfactory work in some of the less-demanding classes, though.

By the end of the school year, he thought his run at Purdue was so over that he planned to join one of the military forces. Then the day of decision came when the Dean sent out the follow-up letter from the first semester. Brodie opened the letter and read it several times, almost as if he didn't understand what the Dean had written.

"It's the same letter," he said to himself with astonishment. "I'm not kicked out."

He put the letter on the coffee table and leaned back on the couch. Thoughts of his childhood with his brother and sister entered his mind. He even remembered the conversation he'd had with Sheila the day he'd headed off to Central State, when she had told him that she wanted him to graduate from college. Brodie took the letter as a sign from her that he had been given another chance. He went over to his desk and grabbed the summer class schedule. As he looked it over, his next-door neighbor came by.

"What's up, Dennis?" Brodie asked as he opened the door.

"You coming to the Kappa graduation party off campus tonight?" Dennis asked. Brodie could tell by Dennis's bloodshot eyes and bubbly demeanor that he had already started drinking. "It's Friday, and school's over. Brodie, my man, we made it!"

"Man, you know I don't get down with the frat boys like that. They worse than bitches. Always running their mouth."

"So, that's a hard or soft no?" Dennis asked with a grin.

They both laughed.

"It's an 'I'm going to bed' type of no."

***

That Friday night, there were graduation parties after graduation parties. It was also the end of the school year for other students, and they partied just as hard as the graduates. At one off-campus party celebrating the graduation of several Kappas were Cymone and her Kappa boyfriend, Raymond. While Raymond and his boys took shots of tequila, Cymone danced by herself in the middle of the dance floor to the song "Livin' La Vida Loca." She'd had several drinks as well but was still able to properly function. When a guy friend approached her and started talking to her, Raymond saw it from the corner of his eye. He started to ignore it, but once he saw his other frat brothers looking at his girlfriend, he knew he had to show everyone who was boss.

Raymond went to the center of the dance floor. His frat brothers followed and brought others along as well to egg on the situation. After a night of drinking, they wanted to see a fight. Raymond being the frat's hothead, they knew he wouldn't disappoint. The moment he got to the center, he pushed away Cymone's friend, who fell hard to the floor.

Her friend quickly jumped up to defend himself. "What's wrong with you, man?"

Cymone tried to jump in between them, but she was held back by Raymond's frat brothers. "Raymond, you don't have to do this!" she cried.

Raymond laughed at her and the situation. He and the friend got nose to nose. "Nigga, you think I'm stupid. You've been trying to holla at my woman since I met her. Unless you are gay or something else, you trying to fuck on the sly. Game recognize game, son."

"It's not even like that," the friend explained.

"You right, it's not even like that, and this shit ends tonight," Raymond said with a smile on his face. "We good."

The friend took a deep breath. "Yeah, man. Cymone is just a friend."

Raymond turned to walk away, but he was stopped by one of his frat brothers, who whispered in his ear, "Don't let that nigga play you. I heard they used to fuck around their freshman year. Got to give that nigga the business."

Raymond turned to face Cymone's friend again. "Take this with you, cuz," he said, and then he started punching the friend in the face over and over until someone came over and broke up the fight. After Raymond was pulled off of Cymone's friend, she ran over and started punching him. Raymond didn't take too kindly to her taking up for the other guy, so he abruptly slapped her across the face. Cymone stumbled back.

"You sticking up for that nigga?" he screamed. "Don't nobody run up on me like that. Nobody."

Cymone cried as her friends consoled her. "He didn't do anything wrong."

"Bitch, stop lying. You and he used to fuck. I ain't stupid."

Cymone began to walk away, but then she came back to him. "You need help. This jealousy you have is just stupid. He's my cousin's boyfriend."

"That don't mean shit to me. Your whole family probably fucked him." Raymond and his boys laughed.

Cymone and her girlfriends dejectedly walked off. She wanted badly to go back and rip his heart out of his chest like he had done her. It hurt her deeply that Raymond was acting like such an asshole. Knowing that he had a compassionate side to him made her feel sorry for him. Though he came from money, she also knew that his family household lacked love and affection. She had given him her heart, and he had crushed it with his constant jealousy and need to control her. But Cymone knew it was now best to move on without him.

***

The next school, Brodie settled down and made straight A's. His GPA recovered somewhat, but by no means was he going to graduate this year with his friends. Though Brodie's roommates had graduated, he knew in order for him to have a chance at graduating next year he had to go to summer school. And that next year graduation still depended on how he did during the summer session.

Besides the investigation into his sister's murder, Brodie had invested a majority of his time into his on and off relationship with Alaina. Alaina was beautiful beyond measure, but was also controlling and selfish. She came from a black aristocratic family and constantly indirectly made mention that Brodie was beneath her. Though she liked the fact that he catered to her every whim. She had come at a time when he just needed someone in his life to distract him from constantly thinking about his sister's death. Though Alaina had committed and admitted to a couple of infidelities during their relationship, Brodie somehow forgave her. Typically, blaming himself for not being there for her needs. And with Alaina's overbearing and self-absorbed personality, he'd forgotten about his own needs and goals and followed her plan for his education. To catch up, Brodie took a full load of five classes for the summer. He knew he had to buckle down and get straight A's to get his GPA back up to respectability. And with Alaina working in Ohio at an internship, he thought it was going to be easy.

On the first day of summer school, as he left the Purdue Student Union and crossed the street, Brodie's wallet dropped out of his backpack without him noticing. When he passed Cymone in the parking lot, he was so focused on getting home that he didn't even bother noticing her along his path. She noticed him, though, because of the Michael Jordan Chicago Bulls jersey he had on. When he got to the end of the parking lot, he could hear someone yelling to him. He stopped and turned and saw Cymone.

She waved at him with something in her hand. "I got your wallet!" she yelled.

Brodie checked his pants, realized what was missing, and rushed back to her. When he got closer, he saw how beautiful Cymone was. He also noticed the skimpy jean shorts and yellow tank top that barely covered her C-cup breasts.

He smiled and grabbed his wallet from her. "Thank you very much. You're a lifesaver. I owe you dinner or something."

She smiled back. "Straight to the first date," she said with a chuckle.

"You got jokes. If I lost my tuition check, my mother would kill me. She works too hard for me to be this forgetful."

"That's great to hear. Single mothers rule the world."

"My mother isn't single. My parents are still together," Brodie said, shaking his head a little bit.

"Well, you said your mother works too hard. You said nothing about your father." Cymone slit her eyes at him. "Your words, dude."

"That's a different story for a different run-in." Brodie put the wallet in his front pants pocket. "What's your name?"

"I'm Cymone." She smiled at him.

"As you already know from my wallet, I'm Brodie."

"That's a very distinct name for a black guy."

Brodie laughed. "My mother thought the name was different and cute."

"Your mother is a smart woman. I like it. But does your girlfriend like it?" Cymone asked to see if he was single. She admired his broad shoulders, dark brown eyes, and thick, luscious lips. His milk chocolate skin was exactly what she craved in a man; though Raymond was light-skinned, this was her preference. She wanted badly to take a bite out of him.

Brodie smiled. "My girlfriend is on the fence. Sometimes I'm not sure if she really likes me. Though she has brought up us getting married in the future a few times, but that's somewhere around her becoming president of the United States."

"Is she white?" Cymone laughed.

"No, she's black. She just has very lofty goals."

"So, you're going to be her Stedman Graham?"

"More jokes, I see," Brodie said with a smirk. "I better go. She's calling me in an hour, so I best be home."

"Okay, but what are you doing tonight after your call?" She saw the look on his face change. "No, I'm not talking about sex, fool."

"Hey, I didn't say that." They shared an awkward laugh.

"I don't have a TV, so it gets boring at my place. I'm taking two classes so that I can graduate in December. What about you?"

Brodie let out some steam. "Man, I still got a year to go. If you want to watch TV at my place, you're more than welcome to drop by. All I do is work. I'm so behind." He took out a piece of paper and jotted down his address and phone number. "Just come by. I gotta go now. My girl is going to kill me if I miss her call."

"You better. Sounds like she might beat you."

"Bye, Cymone," Brodie said, rushing off.

"See ya, Brodie."

As Brodie and Cymone walked away, he looked back at her and smiled, thinking that their interaction had been cute. It also gave him the view of Cymone's incredible body. He thought that Cymone had an interesting, unique style about herself with the homemade ripped, booty-hugging shorts that she had on. In the back of his mind, though, he believed that she wasn't serious about ever coming by his house to just watch TV or anything else, especially after he'd told her about his girlfriend.

***

Later that evening, while Brodie was on the phone talking to Alaina, he heard a knock on his door. He had no idea who it could be outside of his next-door neighbors. His meeting with Cymone had been forgotten at this point. He went and looked out the peephole. To his amazement, it was Cymone. For a moment, he froze, not knowing exactly how to handle the situation.

"Who is that knocking on your door?" Alaina asked.

"The white boys next door. I think they must be drunk tonight," he said, staring at Cymone through the peephole. No way was he going to mention that he had a beautiful woman coming by just to watch TV.

"Just like some white boys on a Wednesday. Are you going to stop them from knocking on your door?" Alaina felt like the knocking had distracted him from giving her his full attention.

"I wasn't going to. I'm tired and was heading to bed anyway."

"Answer the door and then call me back. I want to hear your voice before I go to sleep. I miss you so much."

Brodie smiled. "I miss you, too. Okay, I'll call you right back."

He hung up and opened the door. Cymone had already started walking away.

"Cymone, Cymone, come back," he said, loud enough to get her to stop in the middle of the courtyard.

She looked back at him and smiled. Then she came back to his door and walked in.

"I hope I didn't wake you up or anything," she said, glancing around his apartment.

"No, I was just on the phone with the girlfriend."

"Dang, that's a long time. She must really be special."

"There's two people on that call. I'm special, too," he said. "Women always taking each other's side."

"I'm sure you're special, too, in an education type of way," Cymone said with a laugh.

"You're a regular Queen of Comedy. Lucille Hell Nawl. You do need to watch TV. Probably at home making yourself laugh all night long." He shook his head, smiling.

"Where's the TV, Bernie Lack?" she said glancing around the living room.

"In my bedroom."

"Did you move it there just in case I came by?"

They looked at each other and laughed.

"I guess that would have been a nice player move if I had. Watch a little TV and have the girl fall asleep in my bed."

"So, you're the next Bill Cosby? No means no, Brodie." She grinned at him. "Note to self, don't drink with Brodie."

Brodie smirked. "I was thinking more like what happened to Angela in *Boomerang* at Marcus's place."

"You got *Boomerang*? Now, that's my favorite movie," Cymone said with a giddy look on her face.

"Yep, got the DVD next to the TV. Just stick it in and watch it."

"Are you okay with me watching it in your bedroom?"

"I'm fine with it. I'm not watching it with you."

Cymone seemed a little disappointed that she was going to watch the movie by herself, but she played it off with another joke. "I'm more of a Jacqueline, anyway."

He playfully rolled his eyes. "I would, but I promised my girlfriend that I would call her back."

Cymone laughed. "I guess you weren't able to express your feelings for each other during the three-hour-long call earlier."

"Enjoy the movie, Cymone."

Brodie went back to the kitchen table to grab the phone while Cymone went into his bedroom and started the movie. As he talked to Alaina, he kept looking into the bedroom wondering what Cymone was really about. In a weird way, he even thought that Alaina and her friends were trying to set him up to see what he would do in this type of situation. But since he hadn't bitten on trying to sleep with Cymone, he thought that either Cymone or Alaina would have let him know by this point.

About an hour later, he finished his call with Alaina and went into his bedroom to watch some of the movie with Cymone. She watched it intensely, like it was the first time she had ever seen it. He came in right at the part where Angela and Marcus first kiss. He sat down at the foot of his bed. Neither one said a word during that moment.

"How many ways and how long does it take to say I love you?" Cymone joked.

"Have you ever been in love, Cymone?" he asked, looking at her from the corner of his eye.

There was an awkward pause.

"Actually, yeah," she said as she paused the movie. "I broke up with my boyfriend at the end of the school year. I thought that was love."

"Sorry to hear that. Did you break up because he graduated?"

She chuckled. "That would have been better. That fool hit me."

"Damn, like that? He Ike'd you. You might have loved him, but he definitely thought differently of you. I would never put hands on my woman. I'm really sorry to hear that."

"I'm fine now. Especially now with Ike out of my life." She glanced over at him to see what his facial expression showed.

"Where are you from?" Brodie asked.

"Born in Cleveland, but I was raised in Detroit. My mother and grandmother can't live in the same city or state."

"A Motown chick!" Brodie laughed loudly. "Can you sing? I'm sure you can fight, coming from the D."

She playfully punched him in the arm. "And I will mess you up. Where you from?"

"South Bend, baby, baaabay," Brodie said proudly.

"Why didn't you go to Notre Dame?"

"Too close to home. I needed to get some space from my father."

"I knew it! You got daddy issues, huh?"

"Actually, I do. Me and my father just don't get along at all. It's like he hates me for something. Maybe in a past life, I stole his bike or something. That man is crazy."

"Maybe you should sit down and talk to him and hear what he has to say."

Brodie rolled his eyes. "Let's play the movie."

"I get it. Sorry."

"No big deal. I gave up on him a long time ago. He didn't even come to my high school graduation. And when my sister died, this nigga took his ass to work."

"When did your sister die?" Cymone asked with sympathy in her eyes.

"About a year ago."

She put her hand on his shoulder. "I'm sorry to hear that. That had to be tough. I never lost anybody in my family."

"Really?"

"Yeah, all my grandparents are still alive. Now, I don't know my father, but I've been told he's living with his new family somewhere on the East Coast."

"That's probably for the best. I wish my father was a deadbeat dad."

"Damn. And you two lived in the same household?" Brodie nodded. Cymone finally realized how crazy his relationship was with his father. "Yeah, let's just watch the movie."

As the movie played, they tried to act like they were not thinking about each other, but both were intrigued more than ever now about who the other was deep down inside. Brodie saw compassion in Cymone that Alaina didn't possess, and Cymone saw the perfect guy friend for her during this time in her life. She wasn't trying to find love; she just wanted a good friend of the opposite sex.

When the movie ended, Brodie had fallen asleep. Cymone didn't want to wake him, so she just covered him up and quietly left. As she walked through his kitchen, she saw his journal on the dining table. She looked back into the bedroom, but Brodie was still sound asleep. She casually opened the journal and saw a poem that Brodie had written. She wanted to close it, feeling like she was invading his privacy, but she couldn't because she wanted to know what Brodie was all about, so she read it.

As We Lay

by Brodie Carmichael

Through the white smoke and unleashing of white doves, jumping over a broom to be your groom to eternally have you as my wife is like a dream come true. Sharing laughter, sharing exclusive yet inclusive relations while letting the world know my soul has reached its final destination. My feelings for you are not a revelation, but a fact I have known since I first laid eyes on you. My love for you will never be squandered, and you will know in your heart that a bond like ours need never be pondered. I'm here for life. Wonderful is what you are to me. Forever we will be. My life evaporates without you. Every day, I feel blessed like no other. Whether you are by my side or across the world, I hold you tight. No woman could ever replace you, no matter how many tens she may be. My heart belongs to you until you pour my ashes out over the Red Sea. No matter what others may think, we have something special that is only possible with you and me. This day forward, I love you eternally.

As she stared at the final words again and again, tears fell from her eyes. Cymone couldn't believe he was this passionate. She had felt his words between her thighs and in her heart. Her breathing increased as she looked over the poem again. It was amazing to her that she'd actually met a man who could express himself. Feeling even more guilty, she closed his journal and left his place.

Chapter Three

As the summer school session flew by, Cymone and Brodie grew closer every day they spent together, which was a lot. But their friendship didn't grow romantically; it was totally platonic. They shared their deep inner thoughts, their career aspirations, and some dark secrets. Cymone now felt comfortable with him, but she thought that their relationship wouldn't ever get past the friendship level.

Brodie liked hanging out with Cymone as well, and he always made it clear to her that Alaina was his girlfriend and that they were planning to have a future together. Though Cymone cringed at times when he spoke highly about Alaina like she was some angel from above, she did respect and love his honesty and commitment to his relationship with Alaina.

Cymone knew she wanted a guy like Brodie. Brodie, on the other hand, started to notice the lack of friendship he had with Alaina. They were close; they just weren't as close as he was with Cymone. He still loved her deeply; he just wanted to be able to talk to her about anything. He felt that their conversations were very cold, and they only discussed their relationship as though it were a company merger. Alaina kept the topics at the school, work, and future level. In her mind, anything outside of that got pushed aside as nonsense and died right after being mentioned. Her sense of humor didn't compare to Cymone's at all, nor did she have an adventurous spirit. Brodie knew one thing for sure: Alaina was on a successful track. She had been a driver for him to be better in focusing on his life and future career. To him, success and financial gain outweighed funny and good times. In addition to that, while he had been tumbling through life last year after his sister had died, Alaina had been there to somewhat comfort him.

With the final week of summer school nearing, Brodie studied hard. He wanted to finish strong and get all A's on his report card, but Alaina had also pounded it into his head that he needed to get good grades so that he could land a great job once he graduated.

On Sunday, the start of summer's finals week, Brodie studied at Hicks Undergraduate Library. About two hours into his studying, Cymone came to the library to study, too. From the door, she saw him deep in his books. She smiled as she went over to him. He didn't notice her until he saw a shadow standing behind him. He turned and smiled.

"Cymone."

"Brodie, you are really trying to get all A's, I see." She grinned. "The teacher's pet."

"I have to. The job market for a college grad is hard. Trump is treating black people just like Mexicans. The only difference is that our wall is the border to get opportunities within the country."

"I know. That's why I'm here. I have to get my GPA up so that I can land a job myself."

Brodie pointed at her. "That's exactly what me and Alaina discussed last night."

Cymone cringed. "When is your last final?" she asked, quickly changing the subject.

"Wednesday. Then I have to pack up the whole apartment." Brodie shook his head, stressed about all he still had to do.

"It'll be alright. A couple of drinks, and then you're done. Where are you living next year?"

"Hawkins Grad House. What about you?"

"Young Grad House," Cymone replied back.

"That's cool. We'll be living close to each other."

Cymone smirked. "I would say we could hang out, but I'm pretty sure Alaina will be taking up all of your time."

He laughed her comment off. "No, but it definitely won't be like the summer. She would trip like crazy if I spent that type of time with another woman."

"I wouldn't allow it if I was your girl." She gazed at him. "Maybe Alaina has a Simon in Ohio this summer to entertain her." Cymone chuckled.

"Not funny at all."

"It's only fair," Cymone said with a smirk.

Brodie forced a smile. "Let's talk about something else."

"Will we be friends?" Cymone smiled. "Is that even possible?"

"I do want us to continue to be friends," he said, hoping she felt the same.

"I'm not so sure that would be cool. Does Alaina even know about me?" Cymone looked him square in the face.

Brodie hesitated. He didn't know a way to avoid her question. After about fifteen seconds, he finally said, "Kinda."

"That means no. Brodie, Brodie, Brodie. I get it, though. I don't think I would tell my girlfriend about the hot chick I've been spending time with all summer. Then mention that this hot chick had been in my bed all summer watching movies. And then top it off by saying, 'Nothing happened.'"

He smiled at her. "So, you're the hot chick now."

They both burst out laughing.

"Alaina won't be cool about us. You don't have to pretend she would be. Trust me, women's intuition."

"I guess you see where I'm coming from. I did kinda tell her you existed, but not to the true extent of how much time we spent together or where we spent that time. I basically told her you were like my study partner that I saw in the library all the time. Anything else besides that would have been relationship suicide."

"I get it. Anyway, I hope we still get to see each other next school year. You're a great friend, and I appreciate everything you have done for me," Cymone said sadly, almost like she was saying goodbye.

"Don't make it out to be a funeral. I'll always be your friend. We tight like that." In the back of Brodie's mind, he knew seeing her in the fall would nearly be impossible.

"By the way, are you coming to my end-of-summer-school party on Wednesday night?"

Brodie rolled his eyes. "I wasn't invited to no end-of-summer-school party. Wrong guy," He looked strangely at her and then chuckled to himself. "Sounds like you left me off the first-string VIP list."

"You mean third-string list of scrubs."

"Scrub my ass," he said, turning up his lips.

"You ain't got no car, Brodie."

"You haven't seen me in my best friend's ride on the passenger side," he replied with a smile.

"Anyway, are you coming?"

"Not sure." He didn't want to tell her that he didn't want to be seen with her, especially with the possibility of seeing some of Alaina's friends at the party, too.

She playfully nudged his shoulder. "You want me to beg you, huh?" She really wanted him to be there.

"No, I just need to pack."

"Right, Alaina got another four-hour call scheduled for Wednesday night."

They laughed again.

"I definitely shouldn't have ever shared that with you. That's surely a moment I would like to have back," Brodie said, shaking his head.

"But you did, and I'm going to use it until you die. I got a feeling you are going to die before me." She winked at him playfully.

"Dumb me." Brodie motioned as though he were shooting himself in the head.

Cymone saw some girls she knew come in the library. "My study crew is here. I expect to see you on Wednesday night. Bye."

"Bye," Brodie said nonchalantly, giving her the impression that he probably wouldn't show up.

"You better be there," Cymone gave him the evil eye for emphasis.

"Okay, okay, I'll be there," Brodie replied, pacifying her so she would leave.

Cymone smiled and rushed off to meet with her study crew.

***

Wednesday's party was epic and in full swing when Brodie arrived around ten thirty. Upon entering, he grabbed a beer from the ice chest. His eyes combed the outdoor backyard, searching for Cymone. When he finally found her, she was having a blast hosting what was definitely the party of the summer. Their eyes met, and she immediately went and greeted him with a seductive, though somewhat intoxicated hug. It was obvious she had been drinking, so Brodie didn't read too much into it. But the Cat Woman outfit she had on showed off all her body parts and how fit she was, and that caught his attention as he took several glances down at her.

When Prince's song "1999" came on, Cymone grabbed him by the hand, and they strolled to where others were dancing. After that song finished, they continued to dance and dance, and with each drink, their sexual feelings started to rise. Brodie's hands started off not touching her, but soon he went from her shoulders down to her waist.

Before their dancing moved any further, the music became unplugged. They stopped dancing so Cymone could fix the problem. While she did that and went to the bar to make herself another drink, her ex-boyfriend Raymond showed up to the party. From his bloodshot eyes, it was apparent that he had been drinking, too. Raymond spotted Cymone heading back to the dance area toward Brodie and went to cut her off. Out the corner of her eye, she saw him coming toward her, but she ignored him and kept heading to Brodie. Raymond jumped between them and started to dance with Cymone as if Brodie weren't even there. Cymone stepped back from him.

"What are you doing?" she demanded.

"Baby, I'm back. We can go back to the way it used to be. I still love you. I know you love me." Raymond extended his hand out to her. "We were great together."

Cymone slit her eyes at him. "Are you serious? You hit me and think that I still love you? You don't treat a woman like that."

"I'm sorry," he said, hoping she would sympathize with him. "We can be great together."

She shook her head. "Raymond, please just go."

He didn't want to listen. He began to step closer to her, but within a flash, Brodie was between them.

"She asked you nicely to leave, so leave," Brodie said, balling up his fists. He knew a little about Raymond and how he liked to sucker-punch people, so he stayed on guard.

"Nigga, I should crush you," Raymond said, hoping to intimidate Brodie.

Brodie laughed, knowing he was bigger and more athletic than Raymond. "I'm waiting."

Raymond looked around at the onlookers. He wanted to throw a punch at Brodie, but when he saw that Brodie was ready to fight, he knew Brodie couldn't be sucker-punched. Not being able to do that, Raymond figured the outcome didn't favor him.

"Cymone, I still love you," he said, and then he walked away.

Cymone felt weird about what had just happened. She did still have feelings for him. She just wasn't sure what those feelings were. To hide those unsure feelings from Brodie, she played the incident off with laughter.

"Brothers be trippin'. I need another drink."

Brodie smiled. He could tell she was hiding something, but he opted to not push the discussion. "I can join you in having that drink."

They enjoyed a couple of more drinks, and then the party slowly ended. Before they knew it, they were the only two people left. Brodie started helping her clean her place up, though Cymone insisted she would do it later in the morning. As he cleaned, she continued to play songs. When she played "Have You Ever Loved Somebody" by Freddie Jackson, she wanted him to dance with her.

"Come, Brodie. Take a break and dance."

"We're almost done."

"You gonna leave me hanging. Come on, Brodie," she insisted.

He didn't want to dance, but he went over to her just to pacify the situation. Cymone got close to him and placed her arms around him. Brodie placed his hands around her waist. Cymone then got even closer to him. Brodie smelled her sweet perfume, felt her stiff nipples pressed against his chest, and saw her bare, succulent neck. The music and her body started a rise between his legs. He slowly moved his hands below her waist and onto her butt. Their dancing became more intense. Cymone leaned forward and kissed him on the lips. Brodie kissed her back, adding his tongue to the mix. Seconds later, he pulled away.

"Cymone, I'm sorry. I better go."

"Don't be sorry. I liked it." Cymone didn't want to stop. She thought Brodie was an amazing kisser.

"I shouldn't have kissed you." Brodie was confused by his feelings. "This shouldn't have happened."

"I'm at fault, too."

"I feel like I'm taking advantage of you. I value what we have. I don't want to ruin this friendship."

"Me either. I hope this doesn't change us," Cymone said with passion in her eyes.

"No, I'm good, but I'm going to go now," Brodie replied, leaving right after the words left his mouth.

After the door closed, Cymone dropped down on her couch. She now knew that her attraction to him was real. Though she agreed that she didn't want to ruin their friendship, she also felt that she wanted more from him. What that "more" was, she couldn't define right now. One thing she did want was to move past the kissing they had shared. Thinking about the kiss and beyond brought a smile to her face.

As Brodie walked home, he felt relieved at escaping the possibility of sleeping with Cymone. He had survived the summer without cheating on Alaina. He did want to sleep with Cymone badly, which made him feel guilty for having those feelings. With Alaina coming to pick him up on Saturday morning, he figured that Cymone would forget the moment they had shared and move on like he planned to do. But in the back of his mind, he couldn't let go of seeing her in the catsuit, touching her, and kissing her. It brought a smile to his face as he entered his apartment. Once inside, he immediately took a cold shower to cool himself off.

"Damn Boomerang!" Brodie said as he got out of the shower.

Chapter Four

It was Friday night, around eight thirty. Brodie was on the phone with Alaina as he packed up his things and ate dinner. He was almost done packing. Their conversation was like normal: Alaina discussed her internship and all the things that Brodie needed to do in the coming year so that he could land a great job. And like normal, Brodie was annoyed.

"Can't we discuss something else?" he asked. "What do you want to do for fun this weekend?"

"I'm just trying to make sure we have a successful life together. Successful planning leads to successful results," Alaina said with a smirk.

"Our lives aren't part of a business journal." He rolled his eyes.

"You better not be rolling your eyes, Brodie."

He exhaled. "Of course not. It's been a long week, and I'm tired."

"My baby got straight A's this summer. I'm so proud of you," Alaina said with excitement.

"Thanks. It was a tough summer, but I did it."

"And tomorrow night, when we get back here, you'll be doing it again." Alaina laughed.

"You are so nasty, but I like it. I can't wait to be inside of you again. I'm going to wear you out."

Alaina moaned. "I got so much stress to get out of my system. This has been the hardest thing ever to do. I miss having sex with you."

"I miss it, too," Brodie said as a flash of him kissing Cymone entered his mind. He tapped his head to get it out of his thoughts.

"You are going to be ready when I come tomorrow at 10 a.m.?"

"I'm ready now if you want to come," he replied as he taped up what seemed like the last box.

"I wish I could, babe, but I have to take my roommate to the airport at 8 a.m., and then it takes two hours to get to you."

"Okay, you had your chance to get me early. I still don't understand why Sabrina can't catch a cab."

"You just be ready. See you tomorrow," Alaina said, ignoring his statement about Sabrina.

"Will be. I'll talk to you tomorrow. I love you."

"Love you, too," Alaina said before she hung up.

Coming out of Alaina's bathroom was an athletic built, tall light skinned guy named Jacob. She went over and kissed him passionately.

"About time you got off the phone," Jacob said with a smirk.

"He is my boyfriend."

"Then why are you with me?"

"Testing the waters."

Jacob laughed out loud. "We have done a lot of missile testing this summer. My rocket is worn out."

"Guys do this all the time and they get high-fived. I'm just not sure he's the one." Alaina stared off in the room avoiding eye contact.

"Then why be with him? It's not fair to him."

"I do love him. My parents love him. Everyone expects us to get married. He's a great guy."

"That's not a good reason to get married to someone, especially if you like something else." Jacob pointed down below his waist.

Alaina was getting upset. "Are you my therapist now?" she asked, leading him to her bedroom.

"Okay. Okay. I can't stay long. I have to pack to leave myself tomorrow. Are you still taking me to the airport?"

"Of course."

Brodie was laying on his couch as thoughts of Cymone came to mind again. He shook his head as if that would rid him of the thoughts. The passion that they had briefly shared was dangerous, and he knew that contacting her could ignite a fire that they wouldn't be able to put out, so he had resisted calling her since her Wednesday night party.

Though he didn't know it, Cymone felt the same way, but she didn't have an Alaina to distract her. For her, what they had shared was like sex. Throughout the day and night since their interaction, she would rub her body parts, imagining that it was Brodie. It drove her crazy that she couldn't see him or hear his voice.

After a long deliberation, Brodie felt like he owed it to Cymone to at least say goodbye on the phone. Thinking a phone call was a harmless way to talk to her, he dialed.

Cymone answered, "Hey, stranger." She had a big smile on her face.

"At least I called," he replied with a smirk.

"You got me there. What are you doing?" Her excitement could be heard in her voice.

"I just finished packing. What about you?"

"Bored and drinking. Been playing solitaire most of the night."

"Would offer the TV to you, but I have already cut off the cable and packed up the DVD player. Have you ever played poker?"

"Poker? No. You know how to play?" Cymone curiously asked.

Brodie smiled. "Yeah, I do."

"You should have said you knew how to play card games earlier in the summer."

"My bad. There's always the fall," he joked.

Cymone shook her head. "You and I both know that I'm not seeing you again."

"Damn, you make it sound like our friendship is dying today." He laughed to break the awkwardness of the moment.

"It is," she replied. "Can't you hear us flat-lining? I'm not trying to act crazy, but I enjoyed getting to know you this summer. And I'm sorry, but this does seem like the funeral of our friendship, which tomorrow will be put to rest six feet deep."

He laughed. "I'm going to miss my weird friend from Motown. She was kinda cool." His phone beeped. He looked at the caller ID and saw that it was Alaina. "Hey, Cymone, I better go. I'll see you in the fall. Bye."

Cymone was upset by the abrupt ending to their call. She laughed at the phone to play it off. "I told you it was our funeral. Heading to the hearse now. Bye, Brodie."

Brodie's phone beeped again. "See you, Cymone," he said, clicking over to the other call. "Hey, Alaina."

"Who were you talking to this late?" Alaina asked with suspicion.

"How can you tell?" Brodie asked.

"The phone rings are different when you are on the phone and when you are off. The dial-tone is different. Are you avoiding my question? Don't hide things from me." Alaina wasn't sure about her dial-tone answer, but wanted to find out if he was talking to someone else, so she stuck to it.

Brodie wasn't sure himself if the dial-tone gave off that type of indication when he was on the phone, but not wanting to argue with Alaina he gave her the best acceptable response. "My mother. Why?"

"She's still up?" Alaina asked not really believing him.

Brodie smirked. "Apparently so. Is everything okay, Alaina? I'm surprised you called back."

"What I had to do finished earlier than expected. I couldn't sleep so I called you back. Do you have company over?"

"No."

"You know I refuse to be poor. You will need to go back and get your MBA. My family would be so upset and probably boycott our wedding if we are not a power couple. I want us to be like Jay-Z and Beyoncé."

"What makes you think they got it all made?" Brodie asked. Alaina was starting to work his nerves.

"They are a power couple. Plus, they are crazy rich. Their life has to be perfect."

Brodie sighed. He hated feeling pressured about his future. "Jay-Z isn't perfect. Like every celebrity, he has secrets. And money, though great, doesn't define who you are or how happy you will be. I ain't Hov and Hov ain't me. He got a Billy Goat; I just want a branch from the money tree."

Alaina exhaled. "I see you are in a Brodie mood again. I'll let you go to sleep. I hope you are in a better mood tomorrow when I see you."

In the past, this would have led to them having a deeper conversation that lasted beyond another hour, but Brodie was done with that discussion tonight. "See you tomorrow, love. Bye."

"Is that all you have to say?" Alaina asked, expecting them to argue a little.

"Yep. I need to finish up a few things and go to bed. I'll see you in the morning."

"Bye," Alaina said with anger.

"Bye, Alaina."

Brodie hung up the phone and opened the refrigerator to see what he had to drink. He had nothing. He sat back down and began to write in his journal. As he wrote, his phone rang again. He didn't answer it.

"I've had enough of you tonight, Alaina," he said, letting the phone just ring. As it rang and rang, though, he got madder and madder. He went over to the phone and answered it without looking at the caller ID. "I told you, I—"

"It's me, Cymone."

"Oh, I'm sorry. What's up?"

"Who pissed you off tonight?" She laughed.

"Nobody. What's going on? I thought you were going to bed."

"Do you want to teach me poker?" she asked shyly.

"When?"

"Tonight! This is our funeral. Last time to pay our respects to us," she said as they both laughed.

Brodie raised his brow. "What are you drinking?"

"A cooler. Watermelon flavor. I got some for you, too." She smiled.

Brodie contemplated going over to her place to play poker. He wanted to say no, but he really wanted to see Cymone one last time before he left for the end of the summer. Based on the hesitation she heard in his voice, Cymone anticipated that he would not be coming.

"I'm tired, but I'll come through and show you the rules of poker. You better have them coolers waiting on me. I can't stay long. An hour tops."

Cymone was so happy. "I'll have you back at your place in an hour, promise."

"Okay, give me five minutes," Brodie said, and then he hung up.

As he got his stuff together to leave for Cymone's place, his phone rang. He looked at the caller ID to see who was calling him this late. He saw that it was his mother and immediately picked up.

"Momma, is everything okay?" he asked nervously. He remembered that the last unexpected phone call from his mother had been when she'd called to tell him that Sheila was dying.

"The police said they are closing the case due to lack of evidence. The case is now in their unsolved cases file," his mother said as her voice cracked.

"Which means that unless the evidence comes to them, they are not going to find it. Bastards! Did anybody find the KJ guy? I tried, but nobody knows a guy named KJ in our neighborhood."

"Nope. All they told me was that they have a huge backlog of cases and they have exhausted all their time and resources on the case and have to move on to others. They did return Sheila's items they got from her room. I sent them to you. I don't want to be reminded of anything right now. It's too much for me to handle."

"Man, I miss Sheila," Brodie said, tearing up a bit.

"I know, baby. When are you coming home again?" his mother asked, trying to change the subject. She really missed her son.

"I got all A's this summer."

"Great!"

"Tomorrow, Alaina's coming to get me, and we are going back to her apartment in Ohio to pack up things and bring them back."

Gloria huffed loudly. "I don't know what you see in Alaina. I don't trust her. She thinks she's better than us."

Brodie rolled his eyes. "Momma, Alaina is a great girl. She's going places in life."

"So? That doesn't mean you have to go with her. She's too absorbed in herself and the future. You are still young and don't know anything about love."

"Alaina and I are perfect for each other. We're both flawed and want to grow and build a life together. She's going to be your daughter-in-law one day, so you best get used to it," Brodie said defensively.

"Don't get so touchy. I just want my baby to be happy."

"I am happy."

"I guess that if she's the only woman in your life, I have to deal with it. I will learn to love Alaina."

Brodie's phone clicked. Someone was calling him on the other line. He looked at the caller ID and saw that it was Cymone.

"Is that Alaina calling you?" his mother asked sarcastically.

"No," Brodie said, wishing he hadn't said it after the words came out.

His mother twisted her lips. "And you are in love with Alaina."

"There you go again, trying to start something. That's Peedee."

"This late? What does he want?"

"Duh, I'm on the phone with you. How would I know what he wants?"

"Okay, baby, I'll talk to you later. Have a safe trip tomorrow. And stay out of trouble," his mother said with a smirk. "Goodnight."

"Bye, Momma," Brodie said as he hung up the phone. He stared at it for a few minutes, contemplating what to do about Cymone.

Being a man of his word, he figured that he would go and just leave after a few hands of poker.

It took Brodie exactly five minutes to get to Cymone's place. When she opened up the door, he could smell lavender from the burning candles she had in the living room. She had a cooler in her hand, and about five more were in a small ice bucket on the dining room table. Brodie ogled them.

"You want one?" she asked.

"Seems like I'm way behind and need to catch up," he joked. "Where are the cards at?"

Cymone handed him a cooler and walked over the table and sat down. She wore pink silk pajama pants and a royal blue tight-fitted t-shirt that flaunted her perky breasts. She definitely caught Brodie's eye as he followed her to the table and sat on the barstool across from her. He quickly finished his cooler. Looking at Cymone, he realized he was in trouble. Everything in his mind told him to just leave, but his heart and penis thought differently, so he stayed. He picked up the deck of cards and shuffled as Cymone gave him another cooler.

"By the way, can I borrow your vacuum cleaner? I have to make sure I get my deposit back on this place."

"Sure, but I'll have to get it in the fall," Brodie said with a shrug.

"I guess we don't technically die tonight." She smiled. "We live to see another day."

"I'm booking you on Jimmy Kimble as the opening act." Brodie smiled at her.

"At least I make you laugh."

Brodie took a sip of the cooler. "These are some strong coolers. You sure you're not spiking them?"

"Sure, lightweight."

"Whatever. You sure you ready to learn poker?"

"Deal the cards, fool."

Over the next thirty minutes, Brodie showed her the finer points to playing poker. He also went through two more coolers in the process and was tipsy and playful. Cymone thought it was cute how he couldn't handle his liquor. She laughed at his actions, but she wasn't too far off herself. It became very obvious when she staggered to the refrigerator and grabbed them two more coolers.

"You trying to clown me?" Brodie said, laughing. "You can barely walk."

Cymone made it back to the table. "Made it, fool. I might stumble, but I won't lose."

"Funny girl, you understand the game now?" Brodie asked as he placed the cards back in the deck. "I'm heading home. You gonna get me in trouble."

"I'm harmless."

Brodie exhaled. "I better go."

"So, we're not playing a game? I want to beat the teacher."

He rolled his eyes. "Never gonna happen, Cymone," he said with bravado.

"Don't be scared, little Brodie. Need mommy to call you a ride home?" Cymone kicked him under the table.

"Violence is your method for getting me to stay?" He laughed.

"One game, please, Brodie."

Brodie really wanted to go, but he knew she wouldn't stop badgering him until they played, so he agreed, but only under one condition, which he expected to lead to him being rebuffed quickly.

"Sorry, but I only play strip poker," he said, standing up from the table and readying himself to go. He even put on his jacket.

The room got silent. Cymone perked up as she absorbed what he had just said. She looked at him and smiled.

"Okay, but you have to take off the jacket and shoes. You have way too many clothes on."

Brodie was stunned by her response. He'd expected her to be the responsible one and send him home.

"Are you sure?" he asked, hoping she would change her mind.

"Deal the cards, chicken Brodie," she said. "Don't get scared now."

Brodie took his jacket and shoes off. He even took off his socks, watch, and necklace. "You still can't win, Cymone."

"I'm not losing," she replied with confidence. "I've watched what you do. I got this. No cheating, Brodie."

Brodie guzzled his cooler down. "It's on now."

The strip poker game was oddly intense, as neither one of them knew exactly how far things might go. Brodie, who had never played strip poker, adlibbed on the rules whenever he got stuck. Midway through the game, based on his nervous energy each time she or he had to remove some clothing, Cymone figured out that he hadn't played before. She was nervous, too, but curiosity as to how far they both were willing to go consumed her. As the hands went by and Cymone's clothes disappeared, Brodie became extremely horny. Staring at her shapely, almost naked body only added to his imagination. To catch up with her, he lost several hands of Poker on purpose. The competition finally ended when Cymone had to take off her bra. It was like she was moving in slow motion as she unhooked the back, removed each cup from each breast, and then placed the bra on the table.

Cymone exhaled. "You got lucky."

Brodie tried to not look at her naked breasts. "I won fair and square."

She rolled her eyes as she stood up. "I want to listen to some music." She walked across the room, freely displaying her full assets to him.

Brodie's friend between his legs grew to the point of hitting the bottom of the table. Cymone put on some classic R & B music and then dimmed the lights. The first song that played was 'Love Hangover – the extended version' by Diana Ross. Brodie got up and went and sat on her couch. He still had on his underwear and a baseball cap. Cymone started dancing around by herself. She wasn't drunk anymore and didn't know if she wanted to destroy their platonic friendship. While she danced, the moonlight came piercing into the room through the closed curtain. At that point,

Brodie saw the glimmer of light showing the beautiful flower between her legs. That vision made up his mind, and he wasn't changing it. He was all in.

Cymone still wasn't convinced it was the right thing to do. Brodie did have a girlfriend, whom he had always stated he was committed to, but her feelings for him were very deep. As she danced, she came by Brodie and playfully teased him. She decided to end the night. She was going to be the adult and do the right thing. But then she accidentally stepped on his feet and tripped. Her hand grabbed Brodie's friend to break her fall. It was the best thing and the worst thing that could have happened. His size stunned her. She hadn't thought that Brodie was packing down below the waist like that.

In the darkness, their eyes met. Cymone couldn't let go of his friend. She had to know what it felt like to be inside of her. Brodie slid his hand down her side and grabbed her butt. Feeling his strong hands touching her naked body, Cymone knew that them having sex was moments away from occurring. Not wanting to have kids out of wedlock, she quickly got up and walked to her room. Brodie wasn't sure what her immediate departure meant, he sat there waiting on her to return. Cymone went into her closet and grabbed an unopened box of 12 condoms. She had the box as an emergency if she was to have sex over the summer, which she never thought was going to happen. She took the box back and handed it to Brodie.

"You have a box of condoms?" he asked with a chuckle.

"A girl never knows what may happen. But it's not like it's open."

Tired of waiting, Cymone ripped open the box and passed him a condom. Brodie quickly put it on. Cymone kissed him, and he kissed her back.

"Are you sure about this?" he asked, breathing heavy in anticipation as his excitement was on the verge of an eruption.

"I can't think of a better way for our friendship to die," she said, getting on top of him. "I want you."

Brodie licked and sucked on her nipples.

"I want you, Brodie. Do you want me?" Cymone whispered in his ear as she slowly came all the way down on him. She exhaled in the pleasure the feeling gave her.

Brodie stopped what he was doing. He looked at her. "I know I shouldn't be here, but right now this is the only place I want to be. I know it's greedy of me to want you and to have a girlfriend, but my heart and mind is pointing to you."

Cymone French-kissed him and slowly began to grind on him. The pain of his size was pleasurable as she rode on top. Brodie was shocked that they were actually having sex. Being inside Cymone felt good. It was warm, wet, and amazing. He'd had sex with many women in his life, but this felt like something special. Just hearing Cymone tell him multiple times that she had climaxed within the first ten minutes excited him. At that moment, there was no Alaina; only Cymone consumed his thoughts.

For the next five hours, they made passionate love all over her apartment without taking a break. It was like they were two sex addicts who couldn't get enough of the other. By the time they finished using the last condom, the sun was peeking through the blinds. In the back of Brodie's mind, he knew Alaina was coming to pick him up, but he couldn't get enough of Cymone. She had woken up the inner sexual beast inside of him that had been lying dormant. She was now his "It Girl."

Brodie left Cymone's apartment and went directly to the store for more condoms. He did stop at his place to grab the vacuum cleaner he had promised Cymone she could borrow. When he came back, he and Cymone picked up where they'd left off. It wasn't until Brodie saw that it was nine o'clock that their escapade came to an end. He knew he had to be showered and ready when Alaina came to get him at ten o'clock in the morning.

"I gotta go," he said sadly, looking into Cymone's eyes.

"I know," she said, kissing him. "This was amazing. Brodie, I know you have a girlfriend, and I'm sorry for this happening. I don't want to come between you and her. You are a really good dude. I wish I could find a guy like you."

Brodie kissed her. "You want to find a guy who cheats on his girlfriend?"

They both laughed.

"You get my point. Minus the cheating part. I guess this is bye."

He gazed at her. "Yeah," he replied as he started to get dressed.

Cymone put on her robe and walked him to the door. He kissed her with all the passion he had. She teared up. It was one thing to have a fantastic friendship bond, but now their sexual bond made it even stronger. Tears slowly raced down her face. She knew it would be hard to say bye to him. She just didn't think it would be this emotional.

"Don't cry," Brodie said, placing both hands on her cheeks and kissing her again.

"I won't. You better go," Cymone insisted.

He kissed her one last time and left her doorway. She went back inside and cried some more, knowing now that she had fallen in love with him. And Brodie being with Alaina only added to her heartache.

When Brodie got to his apartment, Alaina was waiting at the door. He didn't know what to say or do as he approached her.

"Where have you been?" she immediately asked.

For a few seconds, all he did was stare at her. Then he thought of what to say. "I went for a quick run."

"I hope you got a lot of sleep last night. I'm tired. You need to drive."

Brodie was dead-tired himself. He knew he had to tough it out. "I'm good. I slept okay last night."

Alaina saw a twinkle in his eye. "You seem happy today. Must have been some good sleep."

He smiled. "Let me take a shower, and then we can hit the road."

"By the way, I grabbed this package you had outside of your door. What do you want me to do with it?"

"Oh, that's from my mother. It's my sister's things that the police returned since they are closing the case for now."

From behind his back, Alaina rolled her eyes. "Make sure you tell your mother hi the next time you talk to her."

"Put the package in your car with my other things. Thanks."

"You don't want to open it?" Alaina asked nosily.

Brodie turned to look her in the eyes. "No, I'm not feeling it right now. Maybe later. It hurts just thinking about it."

"Brodie, you have to eventually get over it."

Steam rushed from his nostrils. "What are you talking about that I have to get over?"

Alaina didn't get it. "You act like I haven't lost somebody in my life before. When I was ten, my dog 'Lady' died. It hurt until my parents bought me another dog."

"What the fuck are you suggesting...that my parents go buy me another sister? Are you hearing the shit coming from your mouth?" Brodie's eyes were fiery red with anger.

"That's not what I'm saying. You are twisting my words. I'm just saying that you need to move on eventually."

"This is my sister you're talking about. I'm never moving on from her. Dead or alive, she's with me."

Alaina saw that Brodie was boiling hot and about to blow. He was typically the calm guy, but right now, he was giving her looks that she had never seen before. "I'm just going to put this in the car and be quiet. I'm sorry for offending you." She turned away from him, rolled her eyes, and went to her car with the box that had been delivered.

Chapter Five

Later that night, when Brodie and Alaina made it back to her place in Dayton, Ohio, she instantly started touching him. With each touch, his mind shifted to the marathon lovemaking session he'd shared with Cymone. He had hoped that with the long drive back to her place, she would be tired and want to sleep herself. The normal Alaina would have followed his current logic. The horny Alaina had other thoughts running through her head. And having not seen her man since the start of the summer, Alaina wanted to get the party started once her front door closed. Though she had sex with Jacob, with Brodie it was more like making love. She wanted the sex and the intimacy afterwards of him holding her in his arms.

As Alaina excused herself from the bedroom, Brodie took it as his opportunity to fall asleep, or at least appear to be. He had nothing left in his tank and knew there was no way he could satisfy Alaina tonight. He tried grabbing his crotch on several occasions, hoping to get some excitement going, but nothing significant happened. When Alaina came back to the room wearing a sexy red silk negligee, he saw her in the mirror attached to the door, and he curled up like a fetus, hoping to get his non-sexual point across.

"I know you're not sleeping on me, baby. It's been too long," she said, cozying up next to him on the bed. "You promised that you were going to wear me out. Those were your words, not mine. I miss making love to you."

Brodie gave her his best "I'm sleeping" impression ever. He didn't move or open his eyes. But Alaina would not be giving up tonight. She got up, went around the bed, and lay in front of him so that they were now face to face. She kissed him and rubbed on his friend between his legs on the outside of his pants.

"Wake up, Brodie," she said, nibbling on his ear. "I want you inside of me."

Brodie acted like he was groggy. "I'm so tired, baby."

Alaina got up and took off the negligee. "You too tired for this?"

Brodie hated trick questions, especially the way she posed them. "No, but I'm just tired. In the morning, I'll be that guy who knocks it out of the park. I promise," he said, hoping the delay would be enough for her to leave him alone for the night.

Alaina got back on the bed and placed his hand on her vagina. "She wants you to knock it out the park now. Tomorrow will just be extra innings."

Flashes of his escapade with Cymone came back to his memory. He missed it. "I'm just so tired," Brodie said with one glance at Alaina.

Alaina gave him a suspicious look. "Is everything okay? Did you meet someone else this summer?"

"No. I love you, Alaina. I'm just tired," he pleaded, hoping that would stop her persistence.

"It's just funny…"

"What's so funny?" he asked, burying his face into his pillow.

"You've never turned down sex in the past, and now you are after we haven't seen each other in two months. Kind of suspicious to me."

"You're blowing this out of proportion. You're the only girl for me. I had a crazy week, and the drive here wore me out."

"Prove it. Hit it from the back," she demanded. She wanted him in the worst way.

"I don't have any condoms," Brodie said, thinking that would save him.

"I got some," Alaina immediately replied, throwing a monkey wrench into his escape plan.

He looked up from his pillow. "You got condoms. Why you got condoms?" he asked, suddenly suspicious.

"I got them at a lingerie party. I got them for you, silly."

"Okay," he said, curling his body up more.

She grabbed his crotch again. "You are really soft. Don't you miss me?"

"Of course, I do," he said. "But today, right now, I'm done. I'm tired."

Alaina didn't hear a word he said. She proceeded to unzip his pants and put her hands on his love muscle. He closed his eyes, and for a few moments, he got hard when images of Cymone's naked body riding on top of him came to mind. Once he heard Alaina's voice again, he went back to being soft.

"Take off your clothes, silly. I don't want to be the only one naked."

Brodie slowly took off his shirt and his pants. He was hoping for some type of miracle to happen that would prevent him from having sex with her tonight. When he was finally undressed, Alaina passed him a condom. He closed his eyes and thought of Cymone. This finally made him hard enough to get the condom securely on.

"Finally. Let's go, Brodie. You move like paint drying."

Hearing her voice, he went soft again. He was limp and shrunk. Alaina didn't care. She bent over.

"I've been waiting all summer for this, baby," she said, putting her head in the pillow as thoughts of her summer with Jacob came to mind.

From behind, Brodie once again closed his eyes and thought of sex with Cymone. Those thoughts did get him mildly hard, and it was enough to get him inside of her. He did his best to please her. Once again, when he heard her voice instead of Cymone's, he quickly went soft. To play it off, he acted like he'd climaxed early.

"Man, that was good." He plopped down on the bed and laid on his back.

"I didn't cum!" Alaina said with attitude. She came face to face with him. "Really, Brodie?"

"I'm sorry, baby, but like I said earlier, I'm tired. And don't you say it."

"Say what?" Alaina fumed.

"That I got some tired-ass dick," he said with a smirk.

"If the dick fits, wear it. Tired is as tired does. No delivery here."

"Damn, harsh words," he said, feeling guilty about his time with Cymone and what it now meant for his relationship with Alaina.

"I'm just saying that I've been wanting you for the past two months, and apparently, you haven't been wanting me during that period of time. I had to beg you to have sex with me tonight."

"Alaina, please, you know how I feel about you," Brodie said, caressing her. "Now you mad because I came and you didn't."

"Actions speak volumes over words, baby. Your actions tonight have told me a lot about us," She slit her eyes. "I love you more than you love me."

"Alaina, that's not true at all."

"I'm not talking about you, per se, but your wayward little buddy. I'm not blaming or accusing, but if your little buddy did sneak into another rabbit hole over the summer, I would understand, and we would just work it out. This is the time to be truthful."

Brodie pondered telling her the truth. Snitching on himself didn't seem like the right thing to do. If Alaina wanted to find out about Cymone and him, she would have to do that work on her own. This moment did give him pause about whether or not he could trust Cymone to keep her mouth shut about what had happened. Cymone being an AKA and having several friends that he hadn't met left a huge doubt in his mind as to whether she was able to keep a secret. He had spent so much alone time with her that he didn't know if she was a blabbermouth or not. He debated all the scenarios in his head and thought coming clean would clear his conscience. He also knew it would be the end of their relationship.

Alaina had dumped her previous boyfriend for cheating on her, so he knew how that storyline would play out. Though it did cross his mind that he didn't dump her when she had cheated on him previously. But Brodie was well aware that Alaina played by a selfish set of rules where she was always the victim.

"Alaina, I'm not cheating on you. We have talked every day and night over and over again about our future. We talked when we woke up and when we went to sleep. There's no other woman but you."

Alaina looked him in the eyes for a long, awkward moment. She knew something wasn't right, but with no evidence, she couldn't convict him of a crime. Brodie's saving grace in her mind was that her friends who had seen him over the summer at Purdue had never mentioned seeing him with another woman. For now, Alaina resolved to move forward with him, but she decided that from now on she would keep a closer eye on him than she had in the past.

She kissed him. "I just don't want to get hurt again." She put her head on his chest. "I'm serious. I think our love could handle you stepping out one time over the summer with someone else and survive. And as long as it was over, I could move on and never think of it again," she added, giving her hunt for the truth one last hurrah.

Brodie did love Alaina. Looking in her eyes, he knew she wasn't done with her investigation of him. He figured that from this point forward, the search for the truth had begun. With school only three weeks away, he feared who Cymone might tell and what she might say. One thing Brodie had in his back pocket was that he was prepared to lie and take it to his grave even if Cymone told the world what they had done.

Brodie looked deep in her eyes. "Our love is real. I don't want to be with anyone else," he said, kissing her. "I want you to be my wife. I want to grow old with you. Have kids with you. All that good stuff."

"I hope you meant it all. I don't want to get married if you have been with another woman."

Brodie gave her a side-eye glance. "Being that you are questioning me about my summer, you can come clean too."

Alaina smiled. "Are you silly? I didn't have time for any of that nonsense. I was an angel. See my wings?"

"That's good to hear."

"We still need to make sure you get a great job after graduation," she said, switching gears back to the normal Alaina.

"I'm on it," Brodie said, trying to instill confidence in her that they were on the same page. "I got all A's this summer."

"This fall, we have to really work hard. I'll talk to Dr. Martin to see if he has any contacts who can look out for you before you get out."

Brodie frowned. "That dude doesn't like me. Didn't you tell me that he thought I was the wrong guy for you and that I wasn't going anywhere in life? He even tried to set you up with another guy in your class, knowing that we are together. I'm good."

"He's not that bad of a person. He's built a good program at Purdue and has mentored several black professionals. Just give him a chance. He's really a nice man."

Brodie chuckled. "He called me a loser, and you think I'm supposed to forget that? I don't think so. Don't worry about me. I'll be fine. I'm graduating from one of the top schools in the country. There'll be plenty of jobs available."

"It always helps to have people like him in your corner," Alaina said, hoping Brodie would soften his stance and change his mind.

He looked at her like she had lost her mind. He couldn't believe she didn't see his point. "Thanks, baby, but I'm going to pass on having a person in my corner stabbing me in the stomach and back." He kissed her and got up. "Want something to drink?" he asked to put an end to the conversation about her mentor. This was a common conversation he had with other black students in the management program, and Alaina was no different. In his eyes, she had drunk the Kool-Aid like the rest of the students who looked up to Dr. Martin like he was a god with magical powers.

"No, I'm okay, but you really need to start your hustle this fall when school starts."

"I will," Brodie said, walking out of the room.

By the door that Brodie had just walked through Alaina saw a used condom package under the chair. She raced to it and quickly disposed of it in the bathroom toilet.

"Shit, that was close. I think Jacob did that on purpose."

As Brodie made it to the refrigerator, he couldn't help but think about how his night would have gone if he'd just had sex with Alaina. He was convinced she would not have been suspicious of him if he had given her the physical intimacy she wanted. He did feel relieved that the summer was over and that he didn't have to see Cymone anymore. Then he looked in the corner and saw Alaina's vacuum cleaner. He thought about just letting Cymone keep his, but it was actually his mother's.

"Damn, Brodie!" he said to himself knowing that he now had to see Cymone again.

Chapter Six

The three weeks before the fall semester started flew by. With school now back in session, Brodie and Alaina looked to strengthen their relationship and get the best grades possible. Their grades were crucial to Alaina's plan of them getting great jobs and being a power couple. Since that night in Ohio, they'd had great times together and grown closer. Even during that period, they'd looked at engagement rings and thought of the best places to live.

Though Brodie seemed to have forgotten about Cymone, he hadn't. Thoughts of that fantastic night were still vivid in his head. He cherished what they had shared, but he felt it was a one-time event that wouldn't be repeated.

Cymone, on the other hand, went home for a week and a half and then returned to school. This being her final semester, she was trying to make it go by as quickly as possible. Since that night with Brodie, she was heartbroken, especially knowing that the next time she might see him, he would probably be with Alaina. And as she was still single, thoughts of Brodie and her were constantly on her mind.

Through the first two days, Brodie and Cymone had yet to cross paths. They both knew it would be awkward when they did, and they wanted it to happen and be over with sooner than later. On the third day, while Brodie and Alaina were walking across campus, he saw Cymone with some of her sorority sisters chatting by the Stewart Center steps. He wanted to avoid seeing her with her friends and avoid Alaina seeing her as well. He attempted to change directions by tugging Alaina to go another way, but she was not buying the change and kept her stride. Brodie was left with no choice, and he continued walking toward Cymone and her friends.

As they got closer, Cymone finally saw him, and her eyes lit up with excitement. She was so focused on Brodie that she didn't see Alaina next to him. Even with her sorority sisters next to her, she waved at him. Brodie saw the wave, but he decided to pretend he didn't see her. After not getting a response, Cymone took a closer look and noticed that Alaina was with him. She realized that he had ignored her because of Alaina, and it upset her that she wasn't going to get a chance to speak with him.

Brodie hoped Alaina didn't notice anything was amiss, but she did.

"Are you okay?" she asked with her eyebrow lifted.

Brodie pretended like he didn't know what she was talking about. "What?" he asked nervously. "Oh, that was the girl named Cymone who I studied with in the library last summer."

"I didn't see any girl."

Alaina quickly blew it off and continued walking as Brodie and Cymone locked eyes. He smiled, and she smiled back. As her smile pierced his heart, his mind drifted back to that marathon lovemaking night. He had prayed that his passionate feelings for Cymone had dissipated, but as his pants bulged out in the center, he realized that wasn't true. He loved her the same as he had that night.

For Cymone, seeing Brodie again was great. She knew any future with him was obsolete. Though the night they had shared had been mentally and emotionally magical, she had departmentalized it as just a moment where her weakness and happiness had met for pleasure. She did miss the laughs and talks with him. Knowing that they would never happen again darkened her mood.

As Brodie and Alaina came closer, Cymone turned away from them. Brodie understood why, but it still hurt knowing that their relationship had turned into such a dark secret. After he passed Cymone, they glanced at one another over their shoulders before turning back around.

Later that evening, when Cymone came back to her dorm, she was surprised to see Brodie waiting in the lobby. Though she was happy to see him, she was still a little upset that he hadn't waved back to her earlier. She walked over to him.

"Who are you waiting on?" she snippety asked.

"My vacuum cleaner. She was supposed to meet me here three days ago. She's gray, about four feet tall, but she cleans up pretty nice." He looked at her, and they both laughed, breaking the tension between them.

"Shoot, my bad, Brodie. I totally forgot about it."

"You been keeping my vacuum hostage since the end of July. Give her freedom," he said with a smirk.

"I should have thrown it away since some people don't like to speak." She slit her eyes at him.

He sighed. "You trippin about today? I'm sorry. I was wrong, and I panicked."

"Panicked, why? Don't nobody want you." She turned her head sideways.

He turned his lips up at her. "So, it's like that now."

"You're not talking about what happened during summer school. It happened. You have a girlfriend, obviously, and I'm focused on graduating in December. Nothing for you to panic about. Our story won't even make the history books. But I did see a small blurb about us in the obituary section right after the death of some people's cat dying."

Her words seemed very heartless as they entered Brodie's ears. For a moment, he took it personally and stared at her, thinking about what to say next.

She read his face and knew he was hurt. "Dang, Brodie, lighten up."

"I'm cool," he said, acting like he wasn't fazed by her remarks.

"Come with me so I can give you your vacuum cleaner," she said as she walked off toward the elevator.

Brodie got up and slowly followed. When they got off the elevator, Cymone went to her room, which wasn't far from it. She opened the door, and they walked inside; Brodie didn't close the door. Cymone went in her closet and grabbed the vacuum cleaner. She handed it over to him.

"So, the summer and us meant nothing?" he asked, staring at her.

Cymone refused to look at him. "What do you want me to say? It was the best summer ever."

Brodie got close to her. "I just want to hear the truth."

"The truth doesn't do any of us any good. You need to move on and just be happy with your girl." Cymone rolled her eyes.

His eyes watered up. "I want to, but I can't get that night or the time we spent out of my head."

"Try harder. I am. This thing we have doesn't do any of us any good. We have to move on."

He shook his head. "It's not that easy."

"What about me, Brodie? I got feelings, too." She stared back at him with the same fire that he was looking at her with. "You think I want to be hurt?"

"I'm not trying to ruin your life, Cymone. I'm not sure what anything means anymore. I just know my truth and that you are the only one in the world I can tell that to."

"You have Alaina."

"Nobody in the world compares to you. You and I know that night changed us both." He got even closer to her and gazed into her eyes. In his heart, Cymone had all the intangibles he desired in a relationship. But after experiencing the hardships of not having much during his childhood, that was a life that Brodie promised himself that he would never see again. And with Alaina coming from a wealthy family, he knew their life wouldn't fall far from that tree. He knew he was wrong trying to have his cake and eat it too, but Brodie didn't how to let either woman go.

Sadness came over her. "Is this about the sex, Brodie? Alaina's not serving you right?"

"Cymone, this is not about the sex. This is about you, me, us. I feel connected to you." He grabbed her hand, but she pulled away. "Don't do this to me."

"You better go, Brodie. This is not what we need."

He exhaled. "I understand. Maybe I got my wants and needs confused. I'll leave you be, Cymone. You have a great semester and life. I'm glad that I got to be a part of it for a brief moment." Brodie grabbed the vacuum cleaner and walked to the door.

Before Brodie started to leave, Cymone closed the door and looked him in the eyes. "I don't want to love you," she said breathlessly.

"I don't want to complicate your life." He grabbed the doorknob. "I won't disturb you anymore. I promise. It was great while it lasted."

Cymone pushed him against the door and then kissed him. Brodie leaned back to look her in the face.

"I'm falling hard for you, Cymone. I better go."

"I haven't stopped thinking about making love to you since the last time. You made my body, my heart feel things I didn't think were possible," Cymone said, getting turned on just remembering how passionate he had made her feel.

Brodie locked the door and swept her up in his arms. He carried her to her bed, and they ripped each other's clothes off. When only her panties were left, Brodie went down and took them off with his mouth. They were soaking wet as her lower body pulsated in anticipation. She thought he might please her orally, but he didn't. If the sex hadn't been so good, Cymone would have kicked him to the curb, but she was too addicted even to think about that now. Brodie put both of her legs over his shoulders, lifted her up in the air, and entered her. It seemed like a continuation of the last time. Their bodies still connected, and their passion for each other poured out with each touch and kiss. Though Brodie had had sex with Alaina since making love to Cymone, it had been nothing like this. He was free and happy to be sweating and holding Cymone. In the back of his mind, he felt she should be the one, but it was hard to forget the strong family background that Alaina's family presented to him. He wouldn't admit it, but he felt that he would have a better lifestyle with Alaina than Cymone.

As Cymone's fingers dug into his body, she whispered, "I'm falling for you, too."

Brodie laid her on the bed and continued making love to her. He came face to face with her. "I don't want to hurt you, Cymone. My feelings for you are real."

"What do we do?" she asked while moaning.

"I just want to love you," he replied, tonguing her down.

The words "I love you" stuck out to Cymone. It was all she needed to hear from him. The last thing she wanted to be was just another piece of booty for him. Knowing how he felt made him having a girlfriend seem unimportant at this time. Any guilt she had beforehand was now washed away since he loved her. She assumed that eventually, he would end it with Alaina.

"And I want you to love me," she said, grabbing his butt and pushing him deeper inside of her. "You feel that."

Brodie and Cymone climaxed at the same time, and then Brodie rolled off her and onto his back. He glanced over and smiled at her.

"When can I see you again?" he asked.

Cymone smiled back. "Do you need your vacuum cleaner today?"

"Not really," he said, and they both laughed.

***

Over the next few months of the fall semester, Cymone and Brodie met often and made love every time. Due to timing and Brodie's girlfriend, their lovemaking happened all over campus in places like study rooms, TV rooms, and even the microwave room at times. Each time, their lovemaking was better, and each time, their bond grew stronger. At times when they were together, the excitement and adrenaline rush of their affair made them forget Alaina even existed. The guilt of cheating did weigh heavily on Brodie, but he kept trying to convince himself that with Cymone graduating in a month, things would fade once she left school.

Cymone, on the other hand, knew she was too deep in her feelings to let go and too deep into the cheating triangle to pressure him now to leave Alaina. Her heart was torn, and though they had promised not to tell a soul of their relationship, she did confide in her sorority sisters, though she didn't reveal who Brodie was by name.

The third end of this triangle, Alaina, was so absorbed in her school work and strategizing her future that she neglected her relationship with Brodie. Though she had snuck off a couple times to go see Jacob at Indiana University in Bloomington, she still loved Brodie, but she took it for granted that he would be there whenever she wanted him. Throughout this semester, they'd hardly spent time together. And when they did, she never wanted to just have fun. Her businesslike demeanor, which she had on all the time, often turned Brodie away, and he would end up in Cymone's arms on most of those evenings. But if you were to ask her, she and Brodie had the perfect relationship, and they were happier than anyone on campus. Her girlfriends felt otherwise and sought out every opportunity to discredit Brodie even knowing Alaina's misdeeds with Jacob. They hated the fact that they had no evidence that Brodie was anything but a loyal and committed boyfriend. Sadly, Jacob did try to persuade her differently, but she never wavered or thought of Jacob in any other fashion outside of just being a sex toy to her needs.

As with most weekdays, Alaina was at the library, studying or hanging out with her girlfriends, and normally, she couldn't have cared less about Brodie's whereabouts, but on this Thursday night, after finishing up her studying with her best friend Sabrina, she felt the need to relieve some pent-up stress. It was unplanned, but with the library being only ten minutes from Hawkins Grad House, she thought it no big deal. When they walked out of the library, it was very cold.

"Are you sure you want to go see him tonight?" Sabrina asked Alaina, hoping she'd change her mind and they go straight to her car and head back to their apartment.

"Girl, I want to have a drink and be with my man tonight."

"Which one?" Sabrina smiled as she rolled her eyes.

"Don't play girl. Somebody might hear you. I know I shouldn't have told you shit."

"Why today? You haven't talked about Brodie all week, and you expect him to jump up and come back to your place just like that?"

Alaina rolled her eyes. "He better. What other purpose should he have?"

***

In the fifth-floor study room of Hawkins Grad House, a naked Brodie and Cymone were having sex. They had closed the door and cut off the lights, but some light did enter the room from the hallway, where the elevators were. It didn't matter to them; Brodie and Cymone were in their sex zone and only cared about pleasing each other. Plus, it was after 10 p.m., and normally, they had the study room all to themselves.

As Cymone bent over the desk, the elevator doorbell rang, and the doors opened. Brodie paid it no mind as he entered her. That all changed when he heard Alaina's voice.

"Girl, I promise you it's only going to take five minutes," she said to Sabrina as they walked by the study room door heading to Brodie's dorm room.

Brodie froze. Cymone looked back at him.

"What's wrong?" she asked, wondering why he had stopped.

"That's Alaina!" he whispered.

"Your girlfriend, Alaina?"

"Yeah, she must be with her girl Sabrina."

Cymone frowned. "Sabrina Thompson, the Delta?"

Brodie shook his head. "Yeah, she's definitely not a fan of mine."

"I don't like her either," Cymone said. "She's a shit starter."

"You did lock the door, right?" Brodie asked as he looked back at the unlocked door knob.

Cymone's eyes focused on the door knob too. "I thought you did earlier when you got the pillows from your room."

"Shit!" Brodie ran to the door and locked it. Before he returned to Cymone, he saw Alaina and Sabrina walking back to the elevator. "They're coming back. Be quiet."

Alaina and Sabrina got back to the elevator. It bugged Sabrina that Alaina was taking Brodie's disappearing like it was no big thing.

"That's interesting. His roommate said that he was in the study room. It looks completely dark to me unless he's in there hiding," she said jokingly. "Brodie, are you in there hiding?"

Alaina stared over at the study room for a second, then walked over to the door and turned the knob. The door didn't open. She put her forehead against the window trying to look inside. Sabrina came over and looked in with her. It was too dark to see anything or anyone.

"This isn't like Brodie to disappear," Alaina said, perplexed by his absence.

"He might be in there sleeping," Sabrina said, cracking a smile. She knocked on the door playfully. "Wake up, Brodie."

"When did they start locking these rooms?" Alaina asked as her eyes scoured the dark room.

Cymone and Brodie both had moved to the other side of the door and could see Alaina and Sabrina's silhouettes looking in. Luckily, they were at the right angle so Alaina and Sabrina couldn't see them.

Sabrina grew tired and walked over to the elevator. "Maybe he went to grab something to eat," she said with a smirk.

"Brodie doesn't like to eat past nine o'clock," Alaina replied.

"I'm not talking about food," Sabrina said with a laugh. "You said he licks the cat."

Alaina ignored her comments. "I'll find him later. He had his chance."

The elevator door opened, and they entered.

Upon hearing the elevator door close, Brodie peeked outside to make sure the coast was clear. He huffed with relief. "That was close." He started to put his clothes back on.

Cymone stopped him. Her adrenaline was too high, and she wasn't going to stop until she was satisfied. "We're not done," she said. "I'm still horny. This is exciting!"

"I thought—"

"No need to think about it now," Cymone said, kissing him passionately.

Brodie dropped his clothes, and Cymone bent over the desk again, but then she stopped and looked back at him.

"I didn't know you ate pussy!" she said.

Brodie was speechless. He didn't think Cymone had been listening to Alaina and Sabrina's conversation that closely. Though they had done a lot sexually, that was the only thing he hadn't done, even though Cymone went down on him often. She'd thought he didn't do the deed, so she'd never pressed him to reciprocate, but now she felt a little cheated.

"I don't," he said.

She smiled, not quite sure she believed him. "You should. Your lips would feel great around my…"

"Maybe in the future," he said, cutting her off.

"I'm going to keep you to that," Cymone said, smiling back at him. "What are you waiting on?" She pressed her butt into him.

Chapter Seven

The day before Cymone's December graduation, she convinced Brodie to join her for dinner on the outskirts of Lafayette. Though they didn't talk about it, it was more of a break-off dinner. Neither one of them expected to see the other again after her graduation. Both were ready to chalk up their time together as only a great time. To ensure they wouldn't be seen, they sat at the back of the restaurant. Brodie, taking extra precaution, sat facing the door. He didn't want to be caught off guard in case someone they knew did come in. Aside from those details, dinner was great. They laughed throughout and gazed into each other's eyes endlessly. From anybody else's viewpoint, they seemed like a couple very much in love. As they finished dinner, Brodie stopped and grabbed Cymone's hand.

"I'm going to miss you," he said with sadness.

"I'm going to miss you too." She flashed a grin that reached her eyes.

"So, what does Cymone's future look like?" he asked.

She grimaced. Not having a job at graduation was a touchy subject for her. "Going back to Detroit and then figuring things out from there. I should have been more serious about finding a job and less horny. But I'll be okay," she said with confidence in her voice.

"I know you will. You're a strong, beautiful black woman. The sky's the limit for you. You might be the first woman president."

"Me against your girlfriend, Alaina. That would be an interesting debate about protecting our borders." Cymone laughed.

"You remembered that? Man, your memory is something else. You remember that but forget what you had for dinner last night."

Cymone smiled. "I wish things had gone differently for us."

"Me, too. I—"

"I know," she said, interrupting him. "It was great while it lasted. I hope for nothing but the best for you in your future. I just hope Alaina makes you happy enough to last a lifetime."

Brodie took a deep breath. He didn't know how to respond. With his intense love affair with Cymone lasting the entire semester, he hadn't thought about his existence with Alaina. He'd only thought about the end game, how Alaina made his future seem bright as a power couple. He decided to avoid the question.

"I wrote something for you."

"Ain't I special," Cymone said sarcastically. Brodie attempted to hand the piece of paper to her. "No, no, I want you to read it."

"Really?" He hated reading out loud to anyone.

"Yeah, that would make it special." Cymone smiled at him. "I'm waiting."

Brodie smirked as he opened up the paper. He looked into her eyes. "Here we go. The poem is titled 'More Than.'"

"Sounds interesting." Cymone cleared a lump from her throat. Based on the title, she expected it to be deep.

Brodie exhaled.

"What started off as a parking lot chat

has evolved to be way more than that.

From your body to your eyes,

I can't forget your thighs,

but it's your conversation

that made me realize you were special.

You opened up my heart

on what love should be.

You opened up my eyes

on truly understanding me.

Though we are heading down different paths,

I hate imagining my world not hearing you laugh.

What we have developed is deep in my soul.

You have grown on me, and those memories, I will keep until I'm old.

In my heart, there will always be a special place for you

laced with flowers and butterflies.

I know tomorrow we will part ways,

but I don't want to lose touch.

I know our situation isn't right,

but in my heart, I love you with all my might.

I know you consider me just a friend,

but to me, you will always be more than."

Tears filled Cymone's eyes as she stared at him, speechless. He had said everything she wanted except for him announcing he was breaking up with Alaina, which, at this moment, she cared even less about. Just hearing that Brodie loved her with such passion and wanted to stay in contact gave her hope that they still had a chance.

"Are you okay?" Brodie asked, breaking the silence.

"I love you, too, Brodie. I just didn't think you felt the same."

Brodie laughed. "I told you before I loved you."

"Yeah, but not that way. I assumed it was the thing you felt you had to say to get some booty."

"You got me pegged as Iceberg Slim. Like I got no heart."

"I didn't say you didn't have a heart, but being that you are still with Alaina and not solely mine, I figured what we have is just an escape for you."

"Is it an escape for you?" he asked, feeling a little hurt by her remark.

"Yeah, of course not. You think I want this type of relationship with anyone. I did this because I love you. But I do know the score of this game and I'm not winning your heart."

"Cymone, I apologize. I don't expect you to understand why I'm still with Alaina when I've spent most of the semester with you, but I do care for her. We have planned out our lives together."

Cymone's nostrils flared up. "No apologies needed. I got my big-girl panties on. I walked into this relationship with eyes wide open."

"I'm sorry. I shouldn't have ever written that poem."

"No, I needed it. That poem might have saved your life. I appreciate hearing what is in your heart. Just knowing your feelings makes me smile."

"I don't want to lose you, Cymone," Brodie said, grabbing her hand.

Cymone slightly pulled her hand back and smiled. "You can't lose what you never had, Brodie. I'll always be your friend, but probably never more than that."

"Ouch," he replied as they both laughed. "Good one."

"On a side note, you are going to be a great songwriter one day. I see you making hits for all the top singers out there. Your future is bright as a songwriter, you know that, right?"

"I don't think so," Brodie said, raising his brow at what he thought was absurd.

"Brodie, you are a talented songwriter. I've looked into your journal. Great stuff."

He frowned. "I guess privacy is not your strong suit."

"I was curious about you. I was pleasantly surprised that you had such a great talent. You can get very deep. I write, too."

"I hope you share it with me one day."

"I will when ready," she said, flicking her hair back.

"That means no." He smiled at her.

"What do you mean?"

"It's your 'tell.' You always flick your hair back when you are nervous or unsure."

"I don't think so." She rolled her eyes.

"Do you think you will have a job within a month?" he asked, staring at her.

Cymone slowly raised her hand to her hair. Suddenly she stopped. "Oh, I hate you. I never realized I did that."

"Really? I noticed that this past summer. You did it a lot."

"Anyway, you are a very talented writer and should pursue it. Your words dig deep into my core. A man who knows how to express himself turns me on. That's partially why we are here today."

"There's no money there starting out. I need to have a job when I graduate."

"Is that your plan or Alaina's?" Cymone grinned at him.

"I don't want to be broke," Brodie said to deflect the conversation. "Do you?"

"This is about you, not me. You can't let someone direct your life. One day, you're going to wake up and see that you hate where you are, and it'll be because it wasn't your plan."

"I'm not going to be like my parents. Alaina is a smart girl, and we have talked about the future. I want the nice house and job."

"Nobody said you shouldn't, but you think you can't get that without her?"

"That's not what I'm saying," Brodie said, getting frustrated.

"All I'm saying to you is that you don't need anybody to run your life. Do it on your own terms. And when you get to the finish line, you'll be happy because you designed the map that got you there."

Brodie was a little put off by her remarks. He knew she was right. He just didn't want to admit it. "It is my plan. I don't want to be a songwriter, period. I wouldn't even know where to start."

Cymone saw the anguish on his face. "I'm sorry, Brodie. I invited you out to dinner to celebrate me, not talk about you."

"Exactly," he replied, glad to move on from discussing his future plans.

Cymone reached into her purse. She handed him a ticket.

"What is this?" Brodie asked, reading the ticket.

"I want you to come to my graduation. At least see me walk across the stage." She smiled.

"I'm not sure that's a good idea." Brodie felt odd about the ask.

"I get it. No guarantees. I really would like to see you there. That's all. But if the risk of someone seeing you there is too great; I understand not taking that risk. I'm not saying sit with my family and pretend to be my boyfriend. I just want to look out into the crowd and see your face."

Brodie thought about it for a brief moment. "Yeah, I'll be there."

Cymone was very surprised that he agreed to come so quickly. She had a whole set of debate points she'd been prepared to argue to get him there. With no debate, she was all smiles. "I know I shouldn't be, but I'm crazy for you."

***

The next evening, during Cymone's graduation ceremony, she looked around countless times in the auditorium to see if she could spot Brodie. As name after name was announced, she became more upset at not seeing him there. With five names to go before hers, Cymone focused on herself and making sure she looked great walking across the stage. Finally, her name was called, and she strutted across the stage and received her diploma. Her family wildly cheered for her. As she made it back to her seat, she looked around one last time, hoping to see Brodie. She couldn't find him.

"Niggas ain't shit," she said under her breath in disappointment.

Backstage, looking at the crowd, was Brodie. He had snuck in and watched the entire ceremony. Though Cymone didn't see him, he had seen her the whole time and had cheered her on as well. He looked at her proudly and with a deeply rooted love.

"She should be the one," he said under his breath. "She is the one. I can't be with Alaina if I'm in love with Cymone."

As the ceremony ended and the graduates went to find their families, he decided he was going to say hi and introduce himself to Cymone's family. He had made up his mind to be with her over Alaina, and he didn't care who saw him. He charged through the sea of people and approached her from behind.

When Cymone turned and saw him, though, it wasn't joy on her face; it was shame. Brodie noticed her weird expression and stopped in his tracks, trying to figure what was going on. Within a matter of seconds, Cymone's family embraced her. Brodie slowly moved forward, but then he stopped again when he saw Raymond, Cymone's ex-boyfriend, step in and give her a big hug and kiss on the cheek. Her family seemed comfortable with Raymond. Cymone stared over at Brodie with sympathy in her eyes, trying to explain things with her glances and eye rolls. Feeling awkward about what he was witnessing, Brodie disappeared back the way he had come.

Chapter Eight

Throughout the winter and spring semesters, Brodie's sole focus was on graduating. Like he had expected, his relationship with Cymone was now in the past, especially after seeing her with Raymond. The fact that she had forgiven Raymond for hitting her disappointed him. Outside of the first two weeks after her graduation, he hadn't heard from her, and he was determined to not contact her either, though his roommate, Steve, had mentioned that a girl had called him several times back in March but had never left a message. In the back of his mind, Brodie assumed that it was Cymone. He just didn't want to reach out to her and rekindle their affair. He figured that if he didn't water it, the relationship would die. He felt that this was the only way for his relationship with Alaina to blossom and grow so that they could have a chance at that future they so often discussed. It had helped: over the past several months leading up to his finals, he and Alaina had become closer, but her badgering about his career and providing her input like it was the law was beginning to wear on him. Brodie was at a crossroads as his graduation day approached. He didn't have a job, nor did his outlook seem bright. Just thinking about life after graduation scared the hell out of him, and the fact that today he would be graduating only made the moment more intense.

As he tried on his cap and gown in his dorm room, Alaina knocked on the door. He looked through the peephole and cringed.

He really didn't want to hear any of her negative comments today. Knowing that she wouldn't leave, he opened the door.

"Hey, babe," she said, entering the room and kissing him on the cheek. She looked at him in his cap and gown. "Aren't you excited?"

Brodie hesitated. The last thing he wanted was to have her go off into the obvious that he was graduating without having a job secured.

He huffed. "I really want to just get this over with. I got more important things to do, like find a job in Denver for us."

Alaina wanted badly to jump in and make her thoughts known again, but she restrained herself, knowing that today was about Brodie graduating.

"It's all going to work out. You will get a great job, I'll graduate, and we'll get married and have beautiful kids." She smiled at him. "It's all part of God's plan."

For the moment, her words put Brodie at ease. This was a rare moment where Alaina hadn't stressed what he hadn't achieved.

"Thanks, sweetheart. Just knowing you have my back is such a great thing. I don't know if I would have made it without you pushing me."

"I told you, we are going to be a power couple like Bill and Hillary."

"So, I get to have a Monica?"

"Not on your life. And don't get me started on that, Brodie. Can't we be Barack and Michelle?"

"Sure." He raised his hands, signaling that he wasn't going to touch that discussion any further. "I better go. My mother and family are downstairs waiting on me."

"Where is your father at?"

Brodie shook his head. "That's what I've been asking myself my entire life. He's never there when you need him to be."

"How does your mother put up with that?" Alaina asked.

"I don't know. I wish she would leave him and see that life can be better. But let's not talk about him. Today is my day. I'm going to try to enjoy it as much as I can. Tomorrow I'm officially an adult."

Alaina kissed him. "I hope my grown adult man remembers he's taking me to South Carolina for my summer internship before leaving me for Denver."

He wrapped his arms around her. "How can I forget? You have reminded me almost every day since you got the internship. I'm going to make sure my baby is safe before I head out to start our life in Denver. I just hope Denver is the right place for us."

"Of course, it is. My friend Tonya is there. Plus, you have your family."

Brodie frowned. "I just hope it's the right place for us."

As he looked in the mirror to make sure he was looking alright, Alaina noticed he had his journal open and had been writing in it. "Are you still writing songs and stuff? I told you there's no career path there. Leave it in your past. We can't afford that hobby in the future."

Brodie closed the journal. "Privacy!"

"We are supposed to share everything."

"I have no problem with that, but not when you going to hate on my writing. That's something I love doing."

"I'm not hating," Alaina said with a smirk. "I'm just protecting my man from heartache."

"Heartache? Writing poems and songs is something I have enjoyed doing since I was a kid. I never thought about making it a career move…"

"Nor should you," Alaina said quickly, in her mind shutting the door on that career aspiration.

Brodie took a deep breath and then exhaled. "We are not having this non-discussion today. I'm not trying to be a songwriter, so there is no point to this continuing. Agreed?"

"Yeah, but—"

"Alaina, not today, please."

"I'm sorry, baby. I just want what's best for you and me," she said, putting her hands on his shoulders gently.

As Brodie looked at her, he said to himself, *you want what's best for you.*

"You ready?" Alaina asked as she slowly walked to the door.

"Let's finish this in style." Brodie strolled over to her, and they walked out.

***

It had been three weeks since Brodie's graduation day, and he still hadn't secured a position or an interview yet. And while he drove Alaina to South Carolina for her internship, he heard it all from her. It was torture to his ears as she brought up all the missed opportunities, classes he should have taken, and comparisons to others who had graduated and were now working. If he could have, Brodie would have gotten out of the car and walked to Denver. Her talks wore down his spirit, and he started to feel dependent on her for guidance. Though she did provide good insight, she also tore down his confidence and made him tentative about what to do next. To mask his weakening ego, Brodie chalked up his difficulty finding a job to having never lived in Denver. He convinced himself that would change once he moved there on a permanent basis.

After about five days of fun with Alaina, it was time for Brodie to catch his flight to Denver. As she and he walked up to the gate, he noticed tears racing down her face. He knew that she loved him, but this was way more emotional than she had ever been before.

"Are you okay?" he asked, holding her in his arms.

"I don't want you to go. What if you stayed here for the summer? I'm going to be lonely without you."

"You have your friend Sabrina coming to see you."

"Sabrina isn't you. She's always starting drama. I really hope she doesn't come. You really should stay. I can tell her that she can't visit."

"I've sent all of my stuff already to Denver. Clothes and TV are already there. Man, I wish you had mentioned this option earlier. I don't want to leave either."

"I don't know how I'm going to survive without seeing you and talking about our future together. This reminds me of last summer."

The moment he'd met Cymone came to mind. Brodie held Alaina close, but he couldn't help but think that what Alaina really was going to miss was her control over him. "I love you, too, baby."

"You make sure you don't find another woman while you're there."

"No one can replace you," Brodie said as another image of Cymone entered his thoughts. "We are meant to be."

The passengers were almost all aboard the plane, and the flight desk attendants were beginning to shut down the gate.

"I better go," Brodie said, kissing her one last time.

"I'm going to try and come see you in July," Alaina said as Brodie pried himself away from her.

"I hope so. Love you," he said, slowly walking away from her.

When the flight desk attendants got ready to close the door, Brodie raced to board. He waved one last time as the door closed and Alaina sobbed.

After the door closed, Alaina wiped her face then grabbed her phone and made a call. "Hey Jacob, what time is your flight?"

***

After being in Denver for a few days, Brodie began to slowly regain his confidence. Alaina not being there to uplift and then tear him down made him think more clearly about what he wanted to do. He'd had several interviews upon his arrival, but most of those jobs were sales related and only paid a commission. Brodie knew he wouldn't be good at pitching products he really didn't believe in. Though he hadn't obtained a job, he had done a lot of writing in his journal, mostly songs about love gained and lost. Cymone had crossed his mind, and he wanted to reach out to her, but he was scared to do it since so much time had passed.

As he prepared for his next interview, Brodie carefully examined his clothes and constantly looked in the mirror as he went over his introduction and how he wanted to look when responding to questions. It was obvious he wanted this job by his persistent pursuit to say the right things while practicing. The interview today was at a radio station as an assistant producer on one of the evening programs. He felt it was the perfect fit for his managing and writing skills. Though he had just spoken to Alaina this morning, he hadn't mentioned the interview to her. He knew that no matter what, she would have been very negative about any job connected to the entertainment industry. He felt that if he got the job first and then told her, she might warm up to the idea that he could still be successful no matter what career path he traveled.

Not having a car, he had his seventeen-year-old cousin Keanna drop him off. He had told her to wait in the car and that he should be done in an hour. From the get-go, when he met the show producers, it was a perfect match. They loved his experience and saw him as a good addition to their team. He also liked their programming style and believed he would be an asset as well. They were having such a great discussion that the interview went over an hour. As they wrapped things up, Brodie and the producers were surprised when

Keanna walked directly into the room and sat down, interrupting them. Brodie was shocked; he had never seen someone do something so asinine. He wanted to crawl out of the room and disappear.

"How much longer are you going to be?" she asked him rudely. She felt no shame in her actions as she sat there like it was the normal thing to do.

The room was silent. It was almost like someone was playing a bad joke on Brodie. The good vibes in the room were now gone. The producers stared at him, trying to get a sense of what was happening. He was at a loss for words as he tried to figure out why she would do the most ignorant thing ever.

He looked at Keanna. "We're finishing up now. Give me a minute."

"Hurry up. I got to be back home before my show come on TV."

"Okay," Brodie responded, grinding his teeth.

Everyone expected Keanna to get up and leave the room, but she just stayed there, waiting for him to finish the interview. Brodie felt it was best to just end his worst nightmare.

"Hey, I'm sorry for what just happened. It was nice talking to you. I just moved here, and I don't have a car yet, nor do I know the bus system. Thanks for meeting with me."

"No problem, Brodie. It was nice meeting you, too," one of the producers said.

Brodie and the producers shook hands. When he walked to the door, Keanna got up and followed him.

At the door, she said to him, "You don't want to work for all these white people. They weren't going to hire you anyway."

Brodie looked at her and shook his head as they walked out the door.

***

Later that evening, Brodie, his cousin Sam, Keanna, and his uncle Big Sam sat in the backyard, talking at Brodie's Aunt's house. Brodie was trying to explain to Keanna how wrong it had been for her to come into the interview. Surprisingly, nobody cared about her actions. Sam and Big Sam were both stuck on the radio station being owned by whites and arguing that he shouldn't be working for someone white. Brodie understood how black Muslims were very pro-black, but he also thought they would understand that the job market was slim and he needed the work.

"First of all, Brodie, you shouldn't have ever gone to that white university. That's where your mind got screwed up," Big Sam said with a chuckle. "Keanna basically did you a favor."

"Man, how you gonna say my mind is screwed up? You don't even know me," Brodie replied, feeling like they were ganging up on him. Growing up in Indiana, Brodie hadn't interacted with his family in Denver that much. It wasn't until after his second year in college, when his sister had died, that he'd met them. But he hadn't met his uncle Big Sam until recently because he had divorced his aunt about ten years ago.

"See, Brodie, I told you. You should have gone to Howard or Morehouse and supported the historical black colleges," Sam said, driving the dagger deeper.

Keanna smirked. "I did you a favor."

Brodie had had enough of their nonsense. "You three are straight crazy. I like to see black people succeed like the next person, but come on. Let's break this down. First thing, for me, going to an HBCU would have only added to my frustration upon graduating and finding out that now I have to go out into a world where I still might have to work for someone other than a black person. I'd be isolated because I have absolutely nothing in common with the non-black person I'm now working with. Secondly, those HBCUs are expensive as well. And lastly, you three are the last ones to be talking about any universities or colleges, since you haven't gone to nor graduated from any. And for anyone to talk about my journey to getting a degree and not even having a journey of their own is crazy. We can't have a discussion about this stuff until you have traveled down my road. Go to school, and then let's talk afterwards."

"If this was my house, I would kick you out," Big Sam said, staring at Brodie. He didn't like the tone with which Brodie spoke to him.

Brodie didn't back down at all. "Too bad this is my aunt's house, so I'm not going anywhere."

His cousin Sam saw the tension between Brodie and his father. He knew both had strong personalities and neither had a problem throwing punches, so he stepped in to end the conflict.

"Hey, Brodie, we still going to go see Dave Chappelle tomorrow?"

Brodie was caught off guard a bit by the quick switch. "Huh?"

"Dave Chappelle in concert. Remember, we got tickets for the show tomorrow."

Brodie smiled. "Definitely. I love me some Chappelle."

Big Sam, feeling out of place, abruptly got up and walked back into the house. Keanna followed. Brodie glanced at them, thinking, *how am I going to live here and deal with them?*

Chapter Nine

At her apartment in South Carolina, Alaina opened the door. On the other side was her sorority sister Sabrina, who, though she was Alaina's friend, was also her fiercest competitor. Every award Alaina had won, Sabrina had wanted to win. From dating to competing for friends, Sabrina wanted to beat her. Alaina was blind to the fact that deep down, Sabrina wanted everything she had. At one time, she'd even wanted Brodie, but he'd chosen Alaina instead. With that rejection, Sabrina had set her sights on destroying Brodie.

Alaina hugged her and welcomed her in. She helped Sabrina with her bags, and then they sat on the couch. Alaina poured her some wine.

"I know you are going to like this. How was your flight?"

Sabrina exhaled. "Tiring."

"If you had just told me when your flight was coming in, I would have picked you up from the airport."

"Don't trip. I was working on something." She smiled.

"Okay. Well, while you are here, my place is yours," Alaina said as they toasted. "Relax and have fun, girl."

Sabrina looked around. "I'm surprised you ain't got a man up in here." She smiled devilishly. "You know my cousin still asks about you. Have you talked to Jacob?"

"Girl, you know I'm with Brodie. But Jacob is fine. He's been here twice since I got here."

"You sure Brodie is with you?" Sabrina asked as she glanced at Alaina.

"Girl, I don't want to hear the drama. You've had it out for Brodie ever since we started dating."

"I just want my girl to be treated right and not be a fool. It doesn't matter what you got on the side. I just…"

"Like I said, I don't want to hear made-up drama," Alaina said as she took a big gulp of wine.

"I'm only talking facts," Sabrina said with her lips twisted in the air.

Alaina rolled her eyes, and Sabrina handed her Brodie's journal.

"Where did you get this?" Alaina asked as she looked sternly at Sabrina.

"You remember that box you had me keep for him? I went through it and found some interesting things that you need to read."

Alaina opened up the journal, and Sabrina began turning the pages to where she wanted Alaina to start reading.

"Start right there. He doesn't love you," Sabrina said, sipping on the wine and leaning back on the couch.

***

At eleven o'clock that night, Sam and Brodie walked into the house. Judging from their laughter, they'd had a great time at the comedy show.

"Nobody is funnier than Dave Chappelle. He's the best comedian right now," Brodie gloated.

"Bigger than Eddie?" Sam asked.

Without hesitation, Brodie replied, "Are you crazy? I love me some Chappelle, but Eddie Murphy is one of the gold standards, right up there with Cosby, Redd Foxx, and Richard Pryor. That's the Mount Rushmore for Comedy."

"What about the Kings of Comedy?"

"What about them? Rest in peace to Bernie Mac, but they not on the Mount Rushmore level," Brodie said, dismissing his cousin's opinion.

"You got Cosby on the Rushmore of comedy?" Sam asked, looking at Brodie like he had lost his mind.

"The US don't take George Washington and Thomas Jefferson off Mount Rushmore for owning slaves, do they? I know you, of all people, agree with that."

"Damn right on that one. We, the people, my ass."

Brodie laughed. "Yeah, the US is built on a bunch of lies and bullshit. This country is real comedy."

"Next. I could go on for days about this country. You don't think Cedric is funny?"

"Yeah, but Steve is the one killing it. He's cleaning up making shows and movies. His shit is endless. Like the male version of Oprah."

Sam stared over at him. "Yeah, but that's going to end one day soon. White people don't like a brother with that type of control."

"Yeah, I see your point, but—"

The home phone rang.

"Dang, who could be calling this late?" Brodie asked.

Sam looked at the caller ID. "Not this area code. It must be your girl."

Brodie grabbed the cordless phone. "Hey, baby, what's up?"

"Who did you go to the show with tonight?" she asked in an interrogating type of way.

"Is everything okay?" Brodie asked, noticing her voice was higher than normal.

"Are you hiding something? Who did you go to the comedy show with tonight?" she asked again, the pitch of her voice rising even higher.

"I went with my cousin Sam. Are you okay?"

In the background, Sam asked, "Is that your girl?"

Alaina huffed as she raised her voice. "Who else would you be talking to at this time at night?"

"Alaina, what are you getting at?"

"Who is Cymone Cartwright?" Alaina asked, anger shooting from her voice.

Brodie stopped breathing. His worst nightmare had come true at the worst time. He thought he'd escaped ever being caught for his indiscretions from last summer and the first semester of last year. On hearing Alaina mention Cymone's name, he knew his house of cards was very fragile. He pondered different things to say, but none of them would save his butt.

Alaina huffed into the phone. "Now you're speechless?"

"I told you, girl. He ain't shit!" Sabrina said in the background. "Writing love letters to this chick like they are married or something."

Hearing Sabrina angered him. "Can we have a private conversation?" he asked. "Take me off speakerphone."

"Why that nigga need privacy now? That's how you started fucking that bitch Cymone! Too much privacy, Brodie!" Sabrina shouted in the background.

Sabrina's comments angered him. "You don't know me like that. You don't know shit about me. Get my name out of your mouth. Alaina, please take me off speakerphone!"

"Brodie, I always knew you weren't good enough for my girl." Sabrina kept pouring salt on the wound.

"Alaina, stop listening to her. She jealous because she doesn't have a relationship like ours. No one even likes her."

"Don't worry about who likes me," Sabrina said, getting angrier. "You're no good, Brodie. Cheater. Loser."

Alaina thought about the fact that Sabrina was single and, with her nosey and petty attitude, had run off every guy who had somewhat liked her. But with this issue, she believed Sabrina; she had concrete proof of what had happened between Cymone and Brodie or so it seemed.

"I don't hear you denying it, Brodie. Did you fuck her or not?" Alaina asked.

Brodie felt like he had been backed into a corner. As the walls caved in on his dream life with Alaina, he knew he didn't want to be remembered for cheating on her. He thought about the words he would use. He didn't want to lie, but also knew he wouldn't survive telling the truth. But with Sabrina in her ear, he knew having a rational conversation about what happened between him and Cymone would happen until he was able to speak with Alaina alone.

"I'm not having this discussion with Sabrina on the call," he said emphatically. "Alaina, I love you, but if you gonna let this miserable woman come between us, then something is wrong with you. Neither one of us is perfect. This is a discussion we should have in privacy."

"Privacy? If I'm so miserable and so dead wrong in what I told Alaina, then why did Cymone tell me herself about screwing you all last summer and in the fall?"

Brodie moved the phone from his face. He wanted to respond to her comment, but didn't this conversation about Alaina and his relationship to be open season for Sabrina to comment about.

"Alaina, can we talk when Sabrina isn't around you?" he pleaded.

"Just tell the truth, Brodie!" Sabrina yelled into the speakerphone.

"Alaina, please get me off the speakerphone," Brodie snapped back. "Sabrina is miserable and wants you to live like her. I love you."

"How do you know her, Brodie?" Alaina asked as she kept him on speakerphone.

"I met her last summer during summer school session. We studied together. I told you about my library friend."

"Was your fuck buddy ever over at your apartment?" Sabrina chimed in with a question of her own.

"Yeah, answer that question, Brodie. Was she ever at your place?" Alaina asked.

Brodie got quiet, and he braced himself for Alaina's response to his answer. "Yeah, she came over and studied."

"Studied my ass!" Sabrina said. "Got him!"

"Damn, quit acting like such a bitch. Can't I just talk to Alaina alone?"

Alaina started crying. "So, you had that bitch over at your apartment fucking her last summer?"

"I said studying! She came by and we studied at my apartment." Brodie said, hoping she would understand the innocence of his time spent with Cymone at his apartment. "You're the woman for me. No one else."

Sabrina huffed in disbelief. "Studying my ass! Girl, you can't believe a word this fool says. Just admit you just got busted Brodie."

"Hey, baby, I'm coming to South Carolina. I need to be with you," he said. "We need to talk with interruption."

"Did you go to her graduation?" Alaina asked, breaking her silence. "Nobody at Purdue knows her so she must have graduated already."

Brodie was stunned by the question. He figured that Cymone had told somebody about them. Not willing to fall on his own sword, he wouldn't admit defeat, at least not on the call with Sabrina present.

"No."

"Quit lying, Brodie!" Alaina said. "I don't trust you anymore. Something isn't right about you or this story. Who did you write this poem titled 'More Than' for? Was it for her? I see her name in the book several times."

"It's just a poem about my feelings," Brodie said hoping she bought his viewpoint.

Sabrina yelled from behind Alaina. "That negro is lying his ass off. That's a poem to get your panties wet and he wrote that because of his feelings. Bullshit!"

"Brodie, I can't do this anymore. My gut tells me you are lying about something. You act like I'm a fool."

"What? So, after all we have been through, it's over like that? Can't we talk it over?" Brodie was shocked that she convicted him with no real evidence or trial.

"This is the bed you created. Now, sleep in it, bitch! Alaina, hang up that phone. He's a straight loser. Dr. Martin said he was."

Alaina wiped the tears from her eyes. "Bye, Brodie."

"Alaina, how many times have I forgiven you?" Brodie asked as his temper rose.

"This isn't about me," Alaina said. "You cheated on me."

"You cheated on me," Brodie shot back. "You are unbelievable."

"If you admit to it maybe we can talk about it, but I'm not standing for all these lies."

Brodie exhaled. He was about to tell the truth until he heard Sabrina whispering in the background. The last thing he wanted was to give Sabrina the satisfaction of being right.

"I just want to be with you. If you would just hear me out," Brodie said as he heard the dial tone in his ear.

Brodie sat there for a long time, just thinking about meeting Cymone and all that had followed. His cousin Sam finally got him to come out of his trance-like state.

"Cuz, you know these chicks are a dime a dozen. She'll be calling you back. You just got to move on for now."

"I think I'm going to LA to start my songwriting career. I got nothing else to lose right now."

"Damn, she got you twisted like that, cuz?" Sam asked, shocked by the quick turn of events of him moving to Los Angeles.

Brodie slit his eyes at Sam. "It's not like that. This is just a sign that I need to focus on me. Alaina will be great. Smart girl, and she has a bright future."

"Sleep on it, and we'll talk in the morning."

"Sam, I'm leaving tomorrow morning."

"You giving up on your girl like that?"

"I only have two moves to make on this chessboard, and one of them still leads to me probably losing. I can go to South Carolina and get rejected or go to LA and roll the dice. At least I got family out there."

"Alaina still loves you, man."

"We'll see in the morning," Brodie said, lying down on his bed to go to sleep. He rolled over, turning his back to Sam, whose bed was on the other side of the room.

"By the way, who is this Cymone chick?" Sam asked. "And did you at least hit it?"

"Goodnight, Sam." Brodie smiled and closed his eyes. "That's a long story, cuz."

"So, you hit it!" Sam laughed.

***

The next morning came swiftly. When Brodie got up, Sam had already left for work. Though Sam hadn't said it, he didn't think Brodie was going anywhere. And he was somewhat right; Brodie didn't know what to do. He loved Alaina and wanted to work it out with her, but he didn't know where to even begin. He went to the home phone and called her. To his surprise, Sabrina answered the phone.

"Can you please put Alaina on the phone?" he asked kindly.

"Unlike you, bum, Alaina has a job. Plus, she's done with you. Be gone already!"

"Sabrina, nobody asked about your commentary."

"Too bad," she said with a happy chuckle.

Brodie shook his head in disbelief. He couldn't believe how Sabrina was disrespecting him. "You know, I've taken a lot of shit from you over the years, and I don't even know why. You're an ugly person on the inside and out. Your hair is jacked up, somebody should have fixed that crooked smile, and maybe you should think about losing a hundred pounds before providing any commentary about shit you don't know about. By your funky attitude, I'm sure you were your daddy's mistake at the lake."

Sabrina yelled through the phone, "I hate you!"

"Okay. I've been hated by better people." Brodie laughed.

"You better stay out there in Colorado if you know what's best for you."

"I'm really scared," Brodie said sarcastically.

"Take your ass back to South Bend, and I'm gonna have my cousin KJ handle that ass."

Brodie froze, thinking about what she had just said. The mention of KJ stunned him. He didn't know how to respond. "Who is KJ?" he asked slowly.

"I see you changing your tone now."

"Who is KJ?" he asked again with great urgency.

"The one who going to put you in your grave if you call me a bitch one more time."

"Where is KJ now? I want to meet him."

"Go to South Bend, and I'll arrange it."

"Sabrina, all bullshit aside, I want to meet your cousin KJ."

"Fuck you, Brodie," she said, and then she hung up. She thought he was playing some type of mind game with her.

Brodie attempted to call her back, but she unplugged the phone to avoid his calls.

He quickly packed his bags, and then he called a cab to take him to the bus station. He wrote his aunt and Sam a thank-you note for their hospitality during his stay and left it on the end table in the living room, but as he was leaving and slammed the front door shut, the note fell and slid under the couch.

As he rode in the cab, Brodie was still thinking about the chess moves he could make. He wanted to fight for Alaina and their future, but he didn't know how he could win her back. And with her mouth, he knew that by now, her family was well aware of what he was accused of. But more important than that was KJ, the person he believed had information about his sister's death. He wished that he could have a normal conversation with Sabrina to find out more about KJ, but with their torrid history, that definitely was not going to happen easily.

When he got out of the cab across from the bus station, Brodie didn't know if he should go to South Bend or South Carolina for answers. And there was always option three: forget about it all and go to Los Angeles to start his music career. He took a deep breath and started to cross the street.

A second later, he was struck by a car. He stumbled over and hit his head on the concrete. He lay on his back, unconscious. A man came over to him and shoved his flashlight in his face. Brodie jumped up like nothing had happened and ran into the bus station.

When he got to the ticket counter at the bus terminal, he decided to purchase a ticket to go see Alaina in South Carolina.

Chapter Ten

Brodie arrived at Alaina's door the next night. He was nervous about what her reaction would be upon seeing him. He was also aware that Sabrina was probably with her. He took a deep breath and then knocked. Alaina came to the door in her pajamas and looked through the peephole. Brodie was the last person she expected to see. In many ways, she assumed that she wouldn't see him ever again unless they crossed paths at a Purdue homecoming event. She slowly opened up the door.

"Why are you here?" she said with her right hand on her hip.

Brodie stood there for a moment, thinking about what to say.

"You came all this way to just look at me?" Alaina asked as she held the door. She wasn't sure if she wanted to invite him in or not.

"No, Alaina, I came all this way because I need to see Sabrina."

Alaina was confused. "Why do you need to see her? You hate her."

Brodie wanted to tell her the real reason about the KJ character, but he didn't want to have Alaina or Sabrina tip KJ off that he was looking for him.

"I just need to clear the air with her. I know you and I may be over, but I don't want it to be because of Sabrina and my relationship."

"Out of nowhere, Sabrina left this morning supposedly going to Spain. She got a job over there or something." Alaina saw the anguish on his face. "Are you going to be okay?"

"I really wanted to talk to her."

"You can talk to me," Alaina said, feeling like Brodie wasn't there for her. "Unless you think our relationship continuing would be a mistake."

"No, I don't think we would be a mistake. I love you, Alaina."

"Then what do you want with Sabrina?" Alaina asked, knowing that it was odd that he wanted to speak to her friend under any pretense.

"She mentioned that she had a gangster cousin from South Bend called KJ. I just wanted to know exactly who he was."

Alaina busted out laughing. "KJ is a he-she. A tranny."

Brodie was shocked to hear it. "A tranny? Are we talking about the same hard-core cousin?"

"KJ is a straight-up hood. I think he was a crack baby." Alaina acted like she had the shivers just talking about it. "Disgusting. What do you want with him?"

"My sister mentioned a KJ before she died. I think it's the same guy."

Brodie stood there, trying to figure things out. Up until now, he'd assumed that KJ was a guy his sister had dated. Finding out that KJ was a tranny screwed up everything he had thought. He didn't know how his sister fit into the puzzle. To his knowledge, she had been straight and never considered anything outside the normal boy-girl relationship. But Brodie began to question whether or not he really knew his sister. He also began to question how far he wanted to take his investigation into his sister's murder. The last thing he wanted was to ruin her image with the rest of his family.

"Well, I do know he's real trouble. He runs the sex trade and drug business from South Bend to Chicago. Supposedly, his boss is in San Francisco. A rich black dude named Derek. Supposedly, black mafia money."

Brodie slit his eyes at her. Alaina seemed to know way more than she should about KJ and his business. "How do you know all this?"

"Sabrina loves to run her mouth. She tried to set me up with KJ. Talking about he's going legit soon. Shit, I must have a stupid sign on my forehead. How a tranny going to please me?"

"I have to meet him."

"Is it worth dying for? I know you love your sister, but KJ isn't stable."

Brodie was apprehensive about meeting KJ and asking him questions, but he felt he needed the answers to understand what had really happened to Sheila.

"I have to do this," he said with determination in his voice.

"KJ might have been the one to pull the trigger. Can you handle that?"

"I don't know, but I'm going to find out. My family needs this."

"The real question is, does your family need to attend another funeral?" Alaina asked. "What about us, Brodie?"

"What are you referring to?" he asked, figuring that she was alluding to Cymone.

"Who is this Cymone girl, really?"

Brodie didn't want to rehash their last conversation or discuss any feelings he had for Cymone with her. To move on, he gave her the response he knew was safe and that Alaina wanted to hear. Mentioning that he still missed and thought about Cymone wouldn't do him any good at this point, especially with Cymone gone from his life.

"Just a girl at Purdue. She didn't mean anything to me outside of being a good friend."

Alaina got tired of standing at the door. "Come inside."

They went and sat on the couch.

"You say she was a girl at Purdue who was a good friend, but nobody even knows her."

Brodie looked at Alaina like she was crazy. "Then how did you find out about her?"

Alaina got up, went to the kitchen table, and came back with a notebook. She handed it to Brodie. "Is this yours?"

Brodie looked at it. "Yeah, but I have my journal."

"Not this one." Alaina showed him the journal she had of his.

Brodie went in his backpack and pulled out the same looking journal. "Dang, same one."

Brodie looked at both journals and noticed that they were identical.

"You have written her name and written poems in the book about the two of you having sex. Sabrina read it, and her imagination went wild," Alaina said rolling her eyes.

"I wrote these poems, that's for real, but there is no name of anyone in this book that is directly associated with these poems. I might have jotted her name down several times as remembering to meet her to study, but that's it."

"I want to believe you, Brodie. I really do, but this seems very weird to me. I want to spend the rest of my life with you, but I can't if there is another woman. We can't love each other unequivocally if you got secrets you can't share. We need to be open and honest even if it hurts."

Her words soaked into his mind. Brodie grabbed her hands and stared into her eyes. He made the decision to finally tell the truth. "There's only you, Alaina. I know I should have admitted earlier, but with Sabrina in the background I couldn't get a word in with you. I'm not with Cymone. I did have feelings for her, but she left Purdue in December. I haven't talked to her or seen her since."

Alaina was shocked by his admission. "Did you sleep with her?"

Brodie looked away. "I did."

"A lot of times?"

"This isn't about quantity. This is about my heart. I had feelings for her and that was it. I take total blame for my actions."

"Do you still have feelings for her?"

"I can't say I do. Like I said I haven't spoken with her since December. She's not something we have to worry about moving forward."

Alaina sighed. She wanted to believe him, so she did. "So, what now?"

"I don't know. Right now, I have to go home and talk to this KJ person. If it's a dead-end, then I'll let it go, and we will never talk about it again. And if you want to be together or not, that's up to you. I definitely would understand if you didn't. I take full blame."

"What about us?" she asked.

"That's in your hands. I love you, but I understand your feelings about me being with another woman."

"I'll wait for you," Alaina said, kissing him on the lips. "Thanks for your honesty."

"I'm tired. Can I crash on your couch until the morning? I want to be in South Bend tomorrow to get this over with."

"Are you going to get the police involved?" Alaina asked.

"I don't think that would be a good idea. I don't want to scare KJ off."

Alaina looked at him and took a deep breath. It was obvious that she needed to address the bigger issue surrounding their relationship.

Brodie saw the intense look on her face. "What is it?"

"You sure you don't still have feelings for this Cymone person?"

A flashback of Cymone and him making love entered his thoughts. Though he still had feelings for her, he knew that wasn't the right answer at this point to give.

""I did, but like I said, that's in the past. She's not an issue for us at all. I don't know how someone got my journal in the first place and then copied it."

"Sabrina found this journal in your boxes. I want to move forward with you, but I won't be involved in some triangle love affair."

"Me either. It's just you and me. There is no Cymone between us."

"Nobody at Purdue even knows who she is."

"She was an AKA."

"Definitely not at Purdue. I checked."

Brodie shrugged. "Are you sure? I saw her studying and going to classes. She even had other study friends."

Someone knocked on Alaina's door, she and Brodie both looked at one another.

"Is that Sabrina?" he asked.

Alaina shrugged her shoulders. "I have no clue," she said as she proceeded to open up the door.

"Surprise!" Jacob said as Alaina fearfully looked back at Brodie. This was her worst nightmare come true.

Brodie stood up and looked at Jacob. He then looked at Alaina again. "I should have known. And you made me feel like I was the bad guy."

"I can explain," Alaina said pleading. "We can still work this out. He doesn't mean anything."

"Bitch," Jacob said. "Unbelievable."

Brodie headed out the door, but stopped as he passed Jacob and Alaina. "This is a good situation for us all. I was tripping thinking that settling for you was the answer instead of finding Cymone."

"What are you saying?" Alaina asked as he walked away.

***

Cymone settled into her coach seat on the plane before takeoff. The flight was from Detroit to San Francisco, and she had a middle seat. As the two people on each side of her bumped her several times as they tried to get comfortable themselves Cymone wanted to scream. She put her headphones on to try to relax and zone out her surroundings, and then she closed her eyes and began to fall asleep. She started to think things were not that bad after all, but then she was brought back to reality by a flight attendant poking on her shoulder. Cymone slowly opened her eyes and looked at her.

"May I help you?" Cymone asked as the flight attendant just smiled at her. Cymone turned the volume down on her headphones.

"You have been upgraded to first class," the flight attendant said, still smiling.

Cymone was shocked. "Upgraded? I didn't ask to be upgraded."

"I know, but a guy in first class just upgraded you."

"Are you serious?" Cymone waited for the punchline.

"Dead serious. I think he has a little crush on you."

Cymone still wasn't sold on taking the opportunity. "Is he cute?"

"Very handsome."

"Is he crazy? I don't want this to turn out to be a Lifetime movie." Cymone laughed at her own joke.

"He appears to be normal to me. He's one of our frequent travelers from the Detroit-to-San Francisco flight. I think he does a lot of business in the Midwest."

"He must be rich." Cymone smiled.

The flight attendant nodded.

"Excuse me," Cymone said as she got up from her seat. She looked at the person sitting in the aisle seat. "Call me Weezy because I am moving on up. Peace!" She gathered all of her things and headed to first-class seating.

When she arrived, she was pleasantly surprised by how handsome and well-polished the man appeared. He was dressed in a beige linen suit with a white linen shirt. He wore sunglasses and had a bald head to compliment his goatee. And even though he was sitting down, she could tell he had a chiseled body. His fair skin had her confused as to what his race was. He definitely was black mixed with something. She just didn't know what. She extended her hand to him.

"Hi, I'm Cymone." She smiled.

He smiled back, and she melted in his hands. He took off his sunglasses to see her beauty, and his hazel eyes mesmerized her even further.

"Hey, Cymone. I'm Derek Winston," he said, grabbing her hand and kissing the back of it. "I'm very glad you accepted my invitation to join me."

She laughed. "I was sitting in coach. It's almost like offering a blind man sight for a day. I get to experience the beauty of people with money."

Derek laughed. "I hope I don't ruin it for you."

"No, but I will say this, though. I love experiencing new things and living on the edge, but there will be no mile-high club going on for me during this flight."

Derek smirked. "Hadn't thought about that in a long time."

"Are you black and Puerto Rican?" she asked, staring at his features.

Derek smiled. "Nope. Black based on how America looks at me, but my family says we're black and Colombian. Is that okay?"

"I was just curious."

"Are you going to sit down, or do you want my fingerprints and DNA?" Derek asked, and they both laughed.

Cymone took the seat next to him and buckled up.

"I guess I should ask if you are married or not." Cymone smiled.

"I'm not," he said, gazing into her eyes. He turned to face her. "I know a beautiful woman like yourself has someone out there in the world madly in love with you. No guy…or girl?" Derek smiled.

"No to both. I lost faith in love."

"Oh, a challenge."

Cymone didn't understand what he meant by that. "What?"

"I hope you give me the chance to give you faith again."

Cymone winked at him playfully. "It's a five-hour flight. Anything is possible."

"You like Champagne?"

"Of course. By the way, what do you do for work, if you don't mind me asking?" Derek seemed too good to be true. And with her recent track record with men, she knew something had to be wrong.

"I own several Wing stops and 7-Eleven stores. And I inherited the money from my grandparents, just in case that was your follow-up question."

Cymone smiled. "You don't know what I'm thinking."

Derek smiled. "I just want to get to know you better. No strings attached."

Cymone raised her brow. "No booty?"

Derek laughed. "You crazy. By the way, do you live in the Bay Area?"

"No, I have a job interview tomorrow."

"You could come work for me?" Derek offered.

Cymone smiled. "Let's just see how things go on this ride first. Baby steps."

***

That evening, KJ was stretched out on his floatation massage chair in his luxury apartment on the waterfront in downtown South Bend. He had on a blue satin dress, which seemed a little long and tight for his five foot eight, two-hundred-pound body. But the color blue looked perfect against his dark chocolate skin. Two white men dressed in black leather jackets and blue jeans came to his door. KJ answered it and invited the men in. They seemed cordial to each other as KJ led them back over to where he had been sitting.

"The boss wants to know if you've retrieved the files from that friend of yours that we had to get rid of?" the taller white man asked in a serious tone.

The question upset KJ, and he got emotional. "First of all, you guys didn't have to kill Sheila. She didn't know anything."

"She knew enough, and she had to go. I don't make up the rules around here. You know how this all goes down."

"It's destroyed," KJ said, hoping to end the interrogation.

The taller white man shook his head. "You have no fuckin' idea what happened to them files. We can't afford any traces of that business coming back to affect our legitimate interests. If you don't have the files, which I know you don't, then I will just have to torture and massacre Sheila's family until we get them back."

"Leave Sheila's family out of this. It's been over three years. If they had something we would know by now. You act like they have been selling time travel on the open market."

"I would, but her mother went snooping, and the boss found out. She contacted one of our police detectives, which was a blessing because, if she had gotten to a policeman who cared about truth and justice, we might have been up shit's creek."

"Just tell him I'll get on it as soon as possible. I promise. The police closed the case for now, and her belongings have been returned to the family. I'll break in and get them, and if it's there, then this situation is over with. But he's overacting. What mother wouldn't want to find out why her daughter was murdered?"

"And if not?" the shorter of the white men asked.

"What are you alluding to?" KJ asked, trying to figure out where the two men were going with their questioning.

The shorter man looked down at KJ. "Maybe you're not man enough for this work, KJ."

Both men laughed.

"You better respect my home," KJ said, eyeing his gun under the coffee table.

"Don't get your panties ruffled, KJ. Just get the files back, and it will be business as usual."

"I'll do my best."

"That's not the winning attitude the boss wants from you."

"I'm not going to kill an innocent family," KJ said, shaking his head. "They don't know anything about this."

The two white men looked at one another.

***

The next night, Brodie arrived in South Bend at his parents' house. Like always, his father was nowhere to be found, though this time, at least, he was upstairs in bed, sleeping. Skipping the pleasantries, Brodie told his mother about finding this KJ person and his thoughts that he was the same person Sheila had befriended as well. His mother was a little nervous about Brodie's plan to approach KJ and ask him who might have killed Sheila, especially after he told her about KJ's current stature in the community as a sex trafficker and drug dealer. She tried to persuade her son not to pursue it any further, but she knew Brodie wouldn't let it go no matter what the cost was at the end.

"I understand, Brodie, that you need to have closure for Sheila's death, but don't you find closure in your death, too," Gloria said, trying to get some sense in his head.

Brodie kissed his mother on the forehead. "I'll be right back."

His mother grabbed him by the arm. "You're not going out there tonight?"

"Why not?"

"Can't it wait until the morning?"

"Momma, it's not going to take that long," Brodie said, hoping to convince her that it would be an in-and-out thing.

"And what if he was the one who killed Sheila?"

"I'm not going to accuse him of anything. I'm just asking questions."

"You keep your phone on," Gloria said, having a bad sense about this whole mission Brodie was on to uncover the truth.

"I will, Momma. See you later."

Brodie grabbed his jacket and walked out the door.

***

About fifteen minutes later, Brodie made it to KJ's waterfront apartment building. When he got to the door, he heard loud music playing inside. He knocked but got no response. He fiddled with the door handle, and the door opened. He slowly crept inside. The music led him to the living room, where he discovered KJ bleeding out on the floor from multiple gunshot wounds. KJ was trying to beg for help, but he couldn't get any words out.

Seeing all the blood gushing out of KJ's body, Brodie froze for a moment. Brodie nervously looked around the place trying to see if the person who had shot KJ was still there. With the coast clear and wanting to help KJ, Brodie tiptoed over to him and tried to stop the bleeding. KJ mumbled something to him.

"I can't understand you," Brodie said as blood squirted on his clothes and face. "I'm Sheila's little brother, Brodie. Who did this to you?"

KJ eyes opened up wide as his breathing got heavier and weaker. Struggling to get the words out, he whispered, "They are coming for your family."

"Who? Why?" Brodie said in a panic. "What is this all about?"

KJ grabbed Brodie by the shirt collar. "You better go," he said before he went into shock.

"What is this about?" Brodie begged, without a response from KJ.

Brodie resumed trying to save his life until he heard someone come in the apartment. He stopped and looked for something to grab so that he could protect himself. He saw a gun under the coffee table, and he grabbed it and pointed it at the living room entry doorway.

It was like he had seen a ghost when Sabrina, Alaina's best friend, entered the room. Sabrina jumped at the sight of the gun pointed at her.

Sabrina saw that it was Brodie. "What are you doing here?" she asked as she noticed the blood all over Brodie's hands and clothes.

"I came to see KJ," Brodie said as tears fell down his face. "I needed to ask him about my sister."

"What are you talking about?" With her eyes on the gun, Sabrina cautiously walked closer to him. Seeing her cousin, KJ, take his last breath, she screamed. "You killed KJ." She pushed the South Bend Police app on her phone to call 9-1-1. She then went to KJ as Brodie stood up and stepped a couple of feet away. He still had the gun pointing at her.

"No, I found him like this. I promise, I didn't do this," Brodie said pleading for her understanding.

"You didn't have to kill him, you monster."

Brodie looked down at KJ and then at all the blood on his clothes. "No, I came here to just ask him some questions."

Sabrina didn't believe him, not one bit. "You are going to die for this." She cried.

"I didn't do this," Brodie said.

"Just like you didn't cheat on Alaina? You're a born liar, Brodie. Put the gun down or are you going to shoot me, too."

Brodie waved the gun at her, trying to tell his side of things, but his actions scared her even more. "Don't be scared, Sabrina. I didn't do this. I found him like this."

Sabrina's eyes stayed focused on the gun. "Please put the gun down."

Brodie was planning on it until he saw evil in her eyes. He knew that if he put the gun down, she would most likely grab it and shoot him with it.

"I can't. You don't believe me."

Sabrina softened her stance. "I believe you, Brodie. I know you're not capable of doing this. It's a misunderstanding that we can explain to the police."

He almost bought her story until he looked out the window and saw about twenty police cars rushing to the building. He looked back at her. "You lied to me."

"I don't like you, Brodie. Never have. You are going to fry for killing my cousin," Sabrina said with KJ cradled in her arms.

Brodie's eyes widened feeling the pressure of the walls caving in. He knew with Sabrina's testimony and KJ being her cousin that no judge or jury would side with his story. He had to escape the scene of the crime now before the police arrested him. He ran into the hallway and noticed that the elevator was coming up to KJ's floor. He also heard the police coming up the stairs. He almost gave up, but then he noticed the laundry chute, and he jumped in it just as the elevator doors opened and the door to the stairwell opened, too.

Police officers swarmed into the apartment with guns drawn. Once inside, Sabrina immediately told them that it was Brodie who had shot and killed KJ. Some of the officers stayed to secure the crime scene, while the others raced out to catch Brodie.

When Brodie got out of the laundry chute, he grabbed some dirty sweats from the pile at the bottom. He quickly changed clothes and escaped through the door to the parking garage. It was a good thing that he hadn't parked in front of the building, because he would have never been able to get to his mother's car, which luckily, he parked two blocks away in an alley. As he sat in her car, he shook nervously. He didn't know what his next move should be. He thought back to his conversations with his mother and Alaina and how both of them had wanted him to just walk away from investigating Sheila's death. He wished he had taken their advice now that he was definitely wanted for murder. He felt trapped; he had nowhere to turn. He knew the police would make sure he couldn't go to his parents' house, or contact Alaina for that matter.

He drove away from the scene and headed up to Michigan. He knew if he stayed in Indiana, they would soon put-up roadblocks preventing him from leaving. It was also in his head that he only had the car for maybe another hour before the police put the APB out on his mother's license plate. Soon after he crossed the county line, he ditched his mother's car. He grabbed her survival kit out of the trunk and walked into the woods with his flashlight.

***

About the same time that Brodie was making his trek through the wilderness of Michigan, South Bend police officers were knocking on his parents' door. Brodie's mother answered the door in her housecoat.

"Yes, officer," she said, hoping that nothing bad had happened to Brodie.

"Have you seen your son Brodie Carmichael recently?" the policeman asked.

"Did something happen to him?"

The officer got mad. "I'm the one asking the questions, ma'am."

"Yeah, I saw him earlier. He went out, and he hasn't come back."

"How does your son know KJ Wright?"

Mrs. Carmichael hesitated. She figured that if she told the police that Brodie had gone to talk to KJ about the death of his sister, it might tell them more than what she wanted them to know. Plus, she still wanted to know why they were looking for Brodie.

"Who the hell is KJ Wright?" Gloria asked, clueless.

"Did your son have any issues that he wanted to resolve with KJ?"

"I'm not answering another question until someone tells me what's going on."

"Ma'am, your son is wanted for murder. He killed KJ tonight at KJ's apartment downtown. When the police arrived on the scene, he fled, I assume, in your car. We already put an APB out. At this point, we want your help to bring him in safely. No need for anyone else to die."

"My son's no killer. If he calls me, I will definitely tell him to contact the police. I swear on my Bible he didn't do this."

"You don't mind if we search the place?"

"Like I have the right to say no," she replied sarcastically.

"Just to be upfront with you, a uniformed officer will be posted in front of your house until we talk to Brodie."

The detective walked out to tell the officers that they could go in to search the premises. As he stood on the porch, the two white men from KJ's apartment looked on from their car.

"Damn, this is not going as planned," the taller one said.

"Boss, isn't going to like this, but at least we're not suspects in KJ's murder," the shorter one replied.

***

Late the next night, Brodie miraculously made it to Pennsylvania. He'd walked and hitchhiked throughout the night to get there. He was cold and very hungry. He always told people he'd grown up rough, but in the last twelve hours, he'd experienced a life that he had never imagined. Creeping through the wilderness, dodging the police, and starving hadn't been what he'd planned on doing when he'd gone to talk to KJ. Just the memory of KJ dying next to him still crept him out. He replayed the events of the night over and over again. He also wanted to know why Sabrina was there when she had told Alaina that she was going to Spain. All in all, he didn't see a way out of this where he came out on top.

When he got dropped off at the rest stop, he went to use the payphone. He made the call with the last change he had in his pocket. On the other end of the phone, the scratchy voice of an older man answered.

"Hello."

"Uncle Benny, it's Brodie. I need your help," Brodie said as he immediately broke down in tears.

Chapter Eleven

The next day, Cymone exited her hotel and jumped in the backseat of a black Cadillac Escalade. Inside, waiting on her, was Derek. They were both dressed business casual. Derek exhaled and smiled as she got in. Cymone was an exquisite beauty to him, but she wasn't a hundred percent sold on him yet. She was attracted to him, but in her mind, she felt that there were some things that Derek had left out about his life. She figured that over time, all his secrets would come to light. She hoped they weren't too dark for her to deal with. He did seem like a cool guy at the moment.

"Hey, beautiful," Derek said, beaming at her. "I'm happy you agreed to have dinner with me tonight."

"What woman is going to turn down the French Laundry?" She laughed.

"See, I thought I was making progress on getting your faith back in love, but I guess a free meal outranks love any day."

They laughed together as the driver took off.

"How was your day?" Cymone asked.

"That's what I like about you. You genuinely seem interested in my day."

"Why wouldn't I be?"

Derek frowned. "You just don't know the type of women I've run into."

"Stop meeting women at the strip club, and you might have a chance at love," Cymone said, playfully bumping his shoulder with her own.

He grinned. "It's just refreshing to meet someone like you. That's all."

"Well, Mr. Winston, you're a very nice guy yourself. I'm glad we met. So, back to your day."

"Well, my day has been very interesting. One of the guys I worked with in Indiana was murdered last night."

Cymone was shocked by the news. "Whoa! Did they catch the guy?"

"No. The guy is on the run."

"Where in Indiana did this happen? I know some people from South Bend," she said with curiosity.

Derek turned to her. "That's where the murder happened. Sabrina, the victim's cousin, told me that it was some guy named Brodie Carmichael who killed him, but she didn't know why. Apparently, she really hates this Brodie guy. He cheated on her friend and based on her crying rant, he's nothing short of the devil."

Cymone didn't know what to say or how to react. She felt like she was smack dead in the middle of what had happened. She remembered Brodie saying something about a KJ person being maybe connected to his sister's death, but that was all. She thought about telling Derek that she knew Sabrina and Brodie, but she didn't want to be involved or have to answer any questions from Derek that he might have about the two of them. She was concerned about Brodie's well-being. Cymone still had love for him. She thought for a moment that she didn't know how to reach him, but then she remembered that he had given her the number to his uncle Benny's place in Pennsylvania. He'd told her that Uncle Benny was the black sheep of the family but that he was the only family he trusted, and if she ever lost contact and wanted to reach him, she should always contact Uncle Benny first. Cymone wanted to stop the car and make the call right then and there, but she knew that would set off an alarm in Derek's head.

"That's deep," she replied with compassion. "Sorry for your loss."

"Thanks. Do you know a Sabrina or a Brodie from South Bend? They went to Purdue," Derek asked.

Cymone shook her head for no.

"Well, that's the gist of my day." Derek poured himself a drink.

"I'll take one of those myself," Cymone said. She wanted to contact Brodie so badly that she felt like she might explode.

"It's strong."

She smiled. "The stronger, the better."

"By the way, what is your last name?" Derek asked. "I was telling a friend last night about this beautiful woman I met on the plane. I told him that you went to Purdue and he did too."

"Legally, Cynthia Jones, but I go by my middle name Cymone and I use my grandfather's last name of Cartwright most of the time. He was my greatest inspiration until he died. Some friends call me C. J., but my close friends just call me Cymone."

"You're not an easy book." Derek smiled.

"Nope. Just great fiction." Cymone winked at him.

"Well, maybe one day I'll turn that last name to Winston."

Cymone chuckled. "I see you got your foot heavy on the gas today."

"Did you hear back about the job?"

She smiled. "I got the job."

"Great news. I hope that means I will be seeing more of you in the future."

"I'm here, you're here, let's see where this ride takes us."

"Are you going back to Detroit this week?"

"Nope. I start next Monday and the hotel is my home for the next month."

"I think you are going to be something special in my life."

Cymone looked in his eyes. "Let's take it slow. I'm not in a hurry. You seem like a nice guy, but I've met a lot of them in my past and they turned out not that nice."

"I'm harmless," Derek said, kissing her hand.

***

The same evening, Brodie woke up in a cold sweat, shouting, "Don't kill my mother!"

His uncle came to his side immediately. "Are you okay, Brodie?" he asked as he sat on the side of the bed.

Brodie was soaking wet. He'd slept miserably, with one eye open, ever since he'd gotten to Benny's cabin in the woods. All he kept thinking about was KJ dying in front of him and being chased by the police. He remembered KJ's dying words that they were coming for his family. Brodie wanted to save his mother and father, but he knew he couldn't reach them with the police tapping the phone lines.

"What am I going to do, Unc?" he asked.

His uncle was just as lost as he was. A military man, he had fought in many wars abroad, but being on the run in America was something he had never trained for. He wanted to help his nephew, but he knew that all he could offer him was the hidden cabin in the woods. Looking into Brodie's eyes, he could tell his nephew wanted his life back.

"I wish I could help you, but I can't. By now, the police have plastered your face everywhere. You can't fly out of the country. And since you left the crime scene, everyone assumes you're guilty and will shoot you on sight."

"I didn't do it," Brodie pleaded.

"I believe you, but what evidence do you have that says differently?"

Brodie sat there, scrambling his brain, trying to come up with some evidence that supported him. Nothing came to mind.

"The gun I held was not the one that shot KJ," Brodie said. "That will prove my innocence."

"The police press conference said today that the bullets that shot KJ matched the gun you had."

Brodie's eyes nearly jumped out of their sockets. "But that was KJ's gun, not mine. I don't own a gun! I don't get this. The real killer must work for the police department."

***

Outside of Brodie's parents' house in South Bend was a police patrol car. The police chief wanted someone stationed outside who would check on the house periodically to make sure Brodie didn't return with them not knowing it first. As the patrolman sat in his car, reading a magazine, the shorter white man who had been at KJ's apartment the night he died knocked on the window.

"Hey, Bob, Captain Jenkins sent me to relieve you."

Bob, the patrolman, looked up at the man. "Hey, Steve, I haven't seen you in years. How's the family?"

Steve smiled. "Great. We just bought a better house up in the hills."

Bob's eyes grew wide. "Somebody's making the big bucks, I see."

"If you apply yourself, Bob, anything is possible. Now, do you want me to relieve you, or should I go back home and get laid."

"Laid? I wish my wife remembered that part of being married." Bob laughed. "My hand is my best friend these days. See you around." Bob drove off.

Steve signaled to someone in the backseat of his car. It was the taller guy from KJ's apartment. The taller guy got out of the car and went around the side of the house to guard the back door while Steve went to the front. Steve knocked on the door.

Gloria answered it. "What now?" she asked angrily. She felt like a prisoner in her own home.

"I need to do a home inspection," he said.

Gloria looked at him sideways. "The other guy came in here less than ten minutes ago. Nothing has changed in that timeframe."

"I could easily take you downtown and book you."

"On what grounds?" Gloria asked with her piercing eyes cutting Steve in half.

"You're hindering an ongoing police investigation. I suggest you let me in so I can do my search before this goes in a direction that you will regret." Steve smiled. "Are you the only one home?"

"Yes, my husband is at work." Gloria started to think something was fishy about Steve. "I would like to speak with your captain."

Steve laughed loudly as his partner quietly approached Gloria from behind and covered her nose and mouth with a handkerchief soaked in chloroform. Gloria was quickly knocked out. The two men carefully searched through the house, looking for a USB drive or any files, but they couldn't find anything at all. They didn't want it to look like someone had broken in so they were neat in their search.

"So, what do we do now, Jim?" Steve asked.

"We take her," Jim replied, "and one of them will give in. Either she will tell us where he's at or he will come looking for his mother. You know how those niggas are about their mothers."

"I'll pull the car around back. You bring her out, and then I'll call it in to the captain in about ten minutes," Steve said. "I'll say she left and didn't come back."

"Good plan," Jim replied with a big grin on his face. "The boss wants us to get this over with soon."

Steve went out to the car and pulled it around to the alley. Jim quickly threw Gloria in the trunk and slammed it shut. Steve walked back inside the house, and Jim followed him back inside. Steve was surprised to see him behind him.

"What's up, Jim?"

Jim pulled out his non-registered gun. "Sorry, but the boss thinks you're the loose end." He then shot Steve two times in the chest. Instantly, Steve died as he fell to the floor. "It's better you, partner, than me."

***

That night, when the eleven o'clock news came on. Brodie's parents' house was the backdrop for the anchor team. The male news anchor opened up the program.

"Tonight, South Bend citizens and the police force mourn the death of Officer Steve Perry, who is now Brodie Carmichael's victim number two! At first, the police thought they could bring him in peacefully, but this time, he killed a cop. The police have contacted the FBI to assist in apprehending him. Like I have said previously, do not interact with this criminal. He now has his mother as an accomplice. My sources tell me that his mother distracted the officer so that he could get a jump on him. Be careful out there."

***

Uncle Benny rushed into the bedroom where Brodie sat by the window, looking out into the woods.

"They got your mother," his uncle said.

Brodie turned to face him. "How can I make this stop? They are going to kill her."

"Just give them what they want."

Brodie threw up his hands. "I don't know what they want."

"It has to be something that they think Sheila had in her possession," Uncle Benny said. "You need to think. Did the police ever return the items that Sheila had in her room?"

A light went off in Brodie's head. "They're with Alaina."

"And, where is she?"

"With some joker in South Carolina," Brodie said, thinking about when he left.

"You need whatever's in that package to save your mother, pronto. And then we have to figure out how to contact them."

"We have to contact Bettie Marshall. That's my mother's best friend. They will contact her knowing that I will contact her, too. Take me to a payphone."

"Let's go. We have to go over to New Jersey. Don't want them pinpointing our location."

"I just wish this had never happened. A time machine would be great right now."

Benny chuckled. "That's what Sheila was working on. Such a bright girl."

"Time machines only work in the movies," Brodie said dismissing his uncle.

They rushed out of the house and jumped into the car. As they drove off, Uncle Benny's home phone rang. On the other end was Cymone, calling from a payphone.

"Damn, Brodie, where are you at?" she said as she hung up the phone.

***

About two hours later, Brodie and Uncle Benny arrived at a payphone in the middle of nowhere just crossed the New Jersey Stateline. Brodie made his first call to Alaina. She answered it nervously because FBI agents were in her house, taping the call.

"Are you cooking tonight?" Brodie asked. Alaina was a terrible cook who hated cooking. He knew her answer would tell him if she were on the police's side or his.

"You know I can't cook. I really need to see you soon. Where are you?"

Brodie shook his head. He knew she was with the police. "Have the police contacted you about me?"

The FBI agents were instructing her how to respond. She looked at the female agent who was writing down the dialogue. "Yes, but they only asked me things about our relationship. Are you coming here tonight?"

Brodie smiled. "Yeah, I'm about an hour away. I lost my key, so please leave the spare under the plant by the door."

"Okay. I really want to talk to/with you about us. I love you Brodie," Alaina said, looking at what the agent had written.

His uncle, who was looking at his watch, signaled for him to end the call.

"I'll see you soon." Brodie hung up.

After he placed the phone back on the receiver, he turned hopelessly to Uncle Benny.

"If I can't get to that package before the police, I'm done. There is no way I survive this with Alaina and the package in her apartment back in South Carolina."

"Then we need to get her out of the apartment. Hopefully, the police will follow, and then we go inside and find it."

"Yeah, but we're in New Jersey, and she's in South Carolina. That won't work. I'm going to have to bluff to get my mother back. If I go to South Carolina and get caught, they will probably kill my mother. If I tell them I don't have what they are looking for, then they'll probably kill my mother. I have to lie."

Back in her apartment, Alaina still had the phone on her ear. It wasn't until she heard the dial tone that she knew Brodie had hung up.

The FBI agents who surrounded her were screaming mad that he'd hung up before they could track his location. They believed that Brodie thought Alaina's place was safe and was coming there as a refuge, so they began to prepare for his arrival.

Back in New Jersey, Brodie called Bettie Marshall. Because he had woken her up, Bettie was mad when she answered the phone, but when she found out it was Brodie, she lit up with joy.

"I know you didn't do what those people are saying in the news. I thought about contacting them and standing up for you. I've known you since you were born, and no way would you harm a fly."

"Thanks, Mrs. Marshall," said Brodie. "That means a lot. I'm calling to see if my mother called you today."

Mrs. Marshall perked up. "That's funny. She just called me about thirty minutes ago, telling me to give you a phone number to call."

"What's the number?"

"It's 574-555-1023. She told me also to tell you she loves you. Is everything okay?"

Brodie sighed. "I hope so, Mrs. Marshall. You have really helped out today. Next time I'm in South Bend, I'm dropping by for dinner. Okay?"

"Definitely. You're just like a son to me, Brodie. Love you. Bye."

"Bye," Brodie said, hanging up quickly. He then dialed the number that Mrs. Marshall had just given him. He and his uncle stared at each other.

Jim answered the phone. "Brodie Carmichael, finally."

"Just don't hurt my mother," Brodie said with pain in his voice.

"That all depends on you, Brodie."

"What do you want from me?"

"We want the file that your sister had, and then you and your mother can go free."

"How am I going to go free? I'm wanted by the FBI. They think I murdered two people. Me giving you this file does nothing for me and my future."

Jim smiled. "At least you save your mother's life."

"How do I get the file to you?" Brodie fumed with anger.

"We can meet in two hours by the entrance of Navy Pier in Chicago."

"I'm nowhere near Chicago. Let's meet in Cleveland in twelve hours."

Jim was impressed that Brodie had made it that far away. "You are more resourceful than I thought. I figured you were living in some mudhole in Michigan, since that's where they found the car."

Brodie didn't want to make small talk. "So, is Cleveland good?"

"Sure," Jim said. "But if you pull any tricks, your mother will be dead on the spot. Do you understand me? No police."

"Aren't you the police?" Brodie shot back.

Jim nodded, impressed. "You aren't as dumb as people think."

"Only a police officer could plant the real gun on the scene. I didn't kill anybody."

"You're right. You didn't." Jim laughed. "See you in Cleveland in twelve hours."

They both hung up.

Brodie looked over at his uncle. "I think he believed me," he said.

"For now, he believes you, but in twelve hours, what are you going to do?"

Brodie stood there, thinking about what the outcome might be. He understood that he was dealing with cold-blooded killers, but he didn't have the luxury of other options to save his mother's life at this time. He wished that there was some way that he could have gotten the items the police had returned from his sister's room. The risk of going to South Carolina and getting caught by the FBI was too much, and it would surely lead to his mother's death.

"We need some guns!" he finally said.

Uncle Benny smirked. "Let's head back to my place, regroup, and then head to Cleveland."

***

Jim and his henchmen gagged Gloria and threw her in the trunk of their car again. They jumped in and drove off. Sitting in the passenger seat, Jim was lighting up his cigar when his cell phone rang. He looked at it and rolled his eyes.

"Yes, boss," he said, answering the call.

"Did you get the files back?" Derek asked. "I need this cleaned up today. This hiccup affects more than just me. It affects the mayor, the governor, and you. Don't think that what happened to Steve, can't happen to you. I got eyes everywhere."

Jim looked at each of the henchmen, trying to figure if they were one of Derek's people planted within his organization. He slowly moved his gun to where it was easily accessible if someone in the car decided to make a move on him.

"I'm meeting Brodie in twelve hours in Cleveland. He has the files, and I have his mother."

Derek smiled. "Make sure they both get two bullets in the head."

"Got it, boss."

Derek sighed. "You know, on second thought, I'm going to meet you in Cleveland."

"I can handle it, boss." By the expression on Jim's face, he didn't want Derek doing his job. He knew if Derek did his job then he would be out of a job and serve no further purpose for Derek.

"Yeah, I've heard that before. Now it's time for some oversight. My flight will arrive in six hours. Be there at the airport."

"I will, boss," Jim breathed heavily as he replied back.

Derek hung up without saying bye. For a few moments, Jim wasn't sure if he were there or not. It wasn't until he heard the dial tone that he realized that he had been hung up on.

"Prick!" He nervously looked at the other guys in the car again.

***

Derek packed his briefcase and left the hotel. As he was riding to the San Francisco Airport, he noticed Cymone calling. He grinned and answered it.

"Hey, beautiful, I was just going to call you. I have to cancel our dinner plans tonight."

"Is everything okay?" Cymone asked with concern.

"One of my businesses in Ohio burned down today. I need to go check on it," Derek said. "But once I'm back, I'm treating you to the weekend of your life."

"Where at in Ohio?" Cymone asked with curiosity.

"Cleveland."

"Oh, man, my grandmother lives there."

Derek was silent for a moment. Finally, he said, "I'm renting a private jet. If you want to come, you can, but I'm not going to be there any longer than a day at most."

Cymone chuckled. "That's the way I go to Cleveland, too. If the King left to go to LA, why would anybody want to stay there?"

"My flight takes off in two hours. I can swing by and get you right now."

Cymone looked around her hotel room, thinking about whether or not she should go. "Okay, I'll be ready," she said joyfully.

***

Back at Uncle Benny's cabin in the woods, he introduced Brodie to his arsenal of guns. Not having much time, they loaded them into the trunk and headed for Cleveland. As the truck rode down the street, Brodie sat in silence, wishing that he had his old life back. His uncle noticed how reserved and scared he seemed.

"Brodie, we are going to get your mother back."

Brodie looked in his uncle's eyes. "I won't be able to live if she dies."

Chapter Twelve

On the private jet headed to Cleveland, Derek was more business-like than when he and Cymone had first met on the plane. It was obvious that something was troubling him. Cymone was like a kid in a candy store. This was her first time on a private plane, and she was enjoying every minute of it—until she saw what she assumed was sadness in Derek's eyes.

She went and sat across from him and grabbed his hands. "I'm sorry things haven't been going your way lately. I'm probably bad luck," she said with a grin.

Derek forced a smile back. "You have been a bright spot in all of this."

"Oh, now that's sweet of you." Cymone leaned in, and they kissed on the lips.

Derek's grin grew bigger. "Maybe I need bad things happening to me all the time if this is what happens at the end."

"No," she said playfully. "I just see that you are not yourself, or at least not the person I met on the plane and had a couple of dinners with. I want happy Derek back."

"You like happy Derek?" he asked as he kissed her again.

Cymone slit her eyes at him. "He's aiight. Nothing special to write home about."

"Will I get to meet your grandmother?" Derek asked.

"I hope you're not going to be upset, but I think it's too early."

"I was just joking with you. We'll split up at the airport, and then I'll call you in about five hours so that we can head back to San Francisco."

"That sounds like a great plan. My grandmother is probably going to die when she sees me on the front porch. It's been a while since I visited."

"I'm glad I could help create that joy."

Cymone hugged him. "You have been a dream come true, Derek. I hope we continue to see each other."

"Nothing is going to stop us," Derek said, giving her a hug and a kiss.

***

As Brodie and Uncle Benny drove past the "Welcome to Cleveland" sign, Derek's plane flew over them. Brodie tried to appear brave, but his uncle could see his hands were shaking nervously.

"You know how to shoot a gun, right?" his uncle asked, looking over at his nephew with concern.

Brodie paused for a second. "Yeah, sort of."

Uncle Benny knew the real answer was no, but it was now too late in the game to divert from their plans.

"Good," he said. "We'll get your mother back, safe and sound. I called in some favors, and these friends know how to handle this type of situation."

Brodie peered over at him. "Just promise me that if it comes down to saving me or her, you'll choose her. I brought this trouble to our family. This is my price to pay."

"Brodie, the price to pay is theirs, not yours. They are going to pay. Once we get your mother back, we will figure out how to clear your name."

His uncle held out his fist, and Brodie slowly bumped it with his.

***

Over at the Great Lakes Shipyard in Cleveland, Jim and his henchmen got in position for Brodie's arrival. He had his men spread out and aim their guns at where the exchange was to take place. Jim got a phone call.

It was apparent from the disdain look on his face that the call wasn't one he wanted to answer, but he did.

"Yes, boss," he said, looking around at the positions that the henchmen were stationed. It crossed his mind that he might be a target as well.

"I'm at the airport," Derek said. "Come pick me up."

"I'll be there in fifteen minutes. It takes that long to get there. You got in earlier than expected?"

"You never know with these flights. Just hurry up," Derek said, and then he hung up the phone before Jim could speak another word.

As Derek was about to make another call, Cymone came out of the restroom on the plane. He greeted her.

"I guess this is bye for now," he said, leaning in and kissing her. "I'm going to miss you."

"It's not going to be that long. Blink, and we will be back on this plane, heading back to San Francisco."

He hugged her tightly. "You make me want to be a different person."

She smiled. "I like the person you are. No need to change."

"Maybe after this, you will consider going to South Africa with me. No strings attached; I just want to be around your spirit."

Cymone pulled away to look him in the face. "Are you okay?"

"Yes, I'm fine."

"Good, my cab just pulled up," she said, kissing him. "Bye, babe."

"Babe? I like it." Derek smiled.

"Bye, boy," she said as she left the plane.

As her cab drove off, Jim and one of his henchmen pulled up in a black SUV. Derek and the three guys he'd brought with him exited the plane. Jim went to the end of the stairs at the bottom to greet Derek as he walked down. Derek had a grim look on his face as he got closer to Jim. When he got to the bottom of the stairs, they came nose to nose.

"You better end this tonight!" Derek said.

"Everything is set up, and I have all the men in place. This Brodie won't know what hit him."

"You better hope not for your sake."

***

At a gas station on the side of the road, Uncle Benny was filling the truck up as Brodie came out of the store drinking a Coke. When he opened up the passenger door to get in, Cymone's cab drove by. She had on headphones but was facing the window. She saw Brodie and was flabbergasted and looked back several times as the cab passed by.

"Turn around!" she shouted at the cab driver.

"What?" the cab driver asked, perplexed.

"Please turn around. That's my friend back there."

"Okay."

The cab driver turned the cab around, but when they got back to the gas station, Brodie and Uncle Benny had left.

"What now?" the cab driver asked.

Cymone looked north, south, east, and west, trying to guess which direction Brodie might have taken.

"North. Go that way," she said, praying that she was right. She reached in her purse and handed the driver two twenty-dollar bills.

The cab driver took off down the empty dirt road. Cymone was on the edge of her seat, looking around to see if she could see the truck that Brodie was getting into. After about ten minutes down the road, she realized that this could not have been the way they went.

"Turn around, please. I don't think they went this way."

The driver turned around and started going back toward the gas station. About midway back, Cymone noticed the truck that Brodie was getting into parked near the airport executive hangar entrance.

"You can drop me off over there," she said, pointing in the direction of the truck.

Without a word, the driver turned the cab and headed that way.

***

Brodie walked over to the old, abandoned warehouse near the river. Uncle Benny was nowhere in sight. Jim, Derek, and their henchmen waited inside the warehouse for him to enter, and once he did, they immediately searched him for weapons.

"Where is my mother at?" Brodie demanded.

"Look around, young buck. You are in no position to bark out orders," Derek said. "Did you look at the files?"

"No. And who are you?" Brodie asked.

Derek turned to Jim and laughed. "Kid is something else." He turned back to Brodie. "Did you tell anybody about this situation?"

"No."

Derek shook his head. "How are we supposed to trust each other if we are starting off with lies."

Derek and Jim pulled their guns out.

"I didn't," Brodie said, confused by what Derek was alluding to.

Derek nodded over at the guy guarding the door near the back of the warehouse. He opened it, and in came Uncle Benny with two men pointing guns at him. He was also tied and gagged. Brodie was speechless. He didn't know what to do next as his eyes went back and forth from Uncle Benny to Derek and Jim.

Uncle Benny looked at Brodie and nodded. Whatever that meant, Brodie was hesitant to do it.

"Okay, I'll do what you want. Kill me and let my mother and uncle go."

Derek sighed. "I'm not going to kill anybody. Give me the files, and you all can go home happily."

Brodie handed him a USB drive. "Can we go now?"

Derek looked at the drive. "So, you made no copy of this or told anybody about it?"

"You think I want this nightmare to continue? I want my life back. I know it won't be easy, but I can't run forever."

Jim went and got Brodie's mother. She and Uncle Benny were put side by side.

"I'm going to check this drive right now, and if it is not the correct file, one of them will die. But I'm going to let you choose," Derek said sinisterly.

As he climbed into the SUV to check the authenticity of the file and its contents, the henchmen brought in Cymone.

Cymone and Brodie locked eyes.

"Cymone," Brodie said, shocked. "Why are you here?"

"I saw you at the store on the way here, and I followed you."

Brodie turned to Jim. "You can let her go. She has nothing to do with this."

Jim laughed. "You do know nobody is safe here."

Brodie didn't quite understand what he meant, but he assumed that it meant they all were going to die. In reality, Jim was still unsure of his own fate.

The henchmen tied and gagged Cymone. She was now next to Uncle Benny and Gloria.

The USB drive was empty. Derek was raging mad as he got out of the car. He didn't see Cymone until after he rushed up on Brodie and punched him to the ground.

"Untie her," he ordered. His men quickly released her. "Cymone, what are you doing here?"

"What is going on, Derek? Is this your business?"

"You know this dude?" Brodie asked.

Derek looked at Brodie and then Cymone. "Is this the dude you were in love with?"

"Derek, please let these people go," Cymone begged.

Derek stood there in disbelief, contemplating his next actions. He had love for Cymone, but power and his business were the two things that he lived for. At best, Cymone could have become a distant third.

"I'm sorry, Cymone. I wish things could have been different. I really did start falling for you."

"It doesn't have to be like this," Brodie pleaded. "We can all walk away and forget about all this. I can disappear. Just get me a passport, and I'll never return to the US. I promise."

Derek rolled his eyes at him. "Less than five minutes ago, you lied to me, and now I'm supposed to believe you? I must have stupid written on my forehead or something for you to believe that I would believe that you could leave this country and never contact or see your momma again. Nigga, please." Derek pulled his gun out again and aimed it at Brodie.

Brodie reached inside his shirt, where the guards hadn't checked, and pulled out a hand grenade. To try to show Derek that he was serious as well, he released the pin. "Looks like we all going to die tonight."

Derek realized that he was too close to escape the impact if Brodie let go. He laughed nervously. "I thought you all searched him. Jim, are these your people?"

Jim was silent. Derek turned his gun on him, and Jim quickly pointed his gun back at Derek. "Not today, boss."

Derek dropped his gun to his side. "I guess you got me."

Before Jim could react, his own right-hand man blew his brains out.

Brodie and the others watched in horror. They now knew that Derek was not stable. He had a deranged look on his face as he looked over at Brodie again.

"I don't think he's serious. Are you willing to kill your own mother?" he asked, shaking his head at him. "You're a person who cares. You're not a killer."

"Better than you killing her. At least I know you'll be dead, too," Brodie said, holding the grenade up in the air. "Don't nobody move."

Derek ignored him and took several steps forward.

"Stop!" Brodie yelled.

Derek stopped and looked over at the men guarding Uncle Benny, Gloria, and Cymone. "Kill the old man."

Within an instant, they shot Uncle Benny, and he died.

In shock, Brodie looked over at his uncle, now lying dead on the ground. He knew Derek was right, that he wasn't a killer, but he also realized that if he didn't do something, they all would be dead.

Derek started aggressively walking toward him again. Brodie stared over at the car behind him. He took a deep breath and then took his hand off the switch on the grenade and counted to four. Everyone, including Derek, froze. Nobody expected Brodie to take that risk.

Seeing that Brodie was going through with it, Cymone grabbed Gloria, and they tried to run away from the explosion. After his count reached four, Brodie threw the grenade at Derek, who tried to escape the impact as well. Brodie raced over behind the car for safety. The grenade exploded, blowing away Derek's legs. Brodie and Cymone both escaped the blast without being hurt. His mother was hurt really bad. As she slowly bled out, Brodie cried, knowing there was nothing he could do to save her life.

"Momma, hold on. Please."

Cymone called 911. Then she comforted Brodie. "Brodie, you have to leave."

"I'm not going anywhere," Brodie said, not wanting to leave his mother's side.

"When the police get here, they are going to take you to jail. You're still wanted for those deaths."

Brodie wasn't trying to hear what she was telling him. "I didn't do those killings."

"I know you didn't. I will tell the police everything, and then we can see what they say. I don't want you to get a raw deal. I know it won't be hard to convince people that he's a crook. But for now, you need to leave."

Brodie's mother died in his arms. He got up and kissed Cymone. At that moment, just before Derek went into shock, he shot Cymone in the back, killing her.

Brodie held her for a moment and then went over to Derek, picked up his gun, and unloaded the remaining bullets into his chest.

Hearing the sirens, Brodie knew he had to run. With everyone dead, he had no proof of his innocence. Even with the real file, it wouldn't prove that he hadn't killed KJ or Steve. He jumped in Uncle Benny's truck and drove off. On the road, he passed many police cars heading to the scene of the crime. He was numb as he remembered how his uncle, his mother, and Cymone had died. He cried profusely. Then a deer came out of nowhere, and he jerked the wheel to avoid it and ran smack dead into a tree.

In the hospital, in a room by himself, Brodie lay unconscious. It was obvious that he had been that way for some time. When the nurse came in and turned on the light, he saw Brodie flinch.

He went closer to him and could faintly hear him trying to mumble something.

"I don't want to live no more," he said lower than a whisper.

The nurse rushed out of the room. Within a few minutes, a team of doctors was around Brodie's bed, waiting for him to say more or do something. It took a couple of days, but finally, Brodie started to come out of his coma.

When he opened his eyes, he was mesmerized by the many faces staring at him. He was so weak he couldn't express his discontent with them being there like that. Several of the medical staff checked and double-checked his vitals. The nurse brought him water, which he appreciated immensely, and he gestured for more. Still weak, he fell back to sleep.

Later that night, the hospital was quiet. Brodie, though still weak, struggled to get out of bed. He looked out into the hallway and saw that everyone was either sleeping or attending to patients. He went back to his bed.

"I don't want to spend the rest of my life in prison. I got to go," he said to himself. He slowly went into the closet, but it was empty. "No clothes aren't going to stop me. Why was I not handcuffed?"

He crept slowly down the hospital hallway. He would duck into rooms when he saw medical staff coming. When he got to the stairs, he said a silent prayer to himself, hoping that he could make it down to exit the building. It took a long time, but he finally made it out.

As he walked through the parking lot, he realized that he was back in South Bend, Indiana, but it wasn't actually a hospital he was escaping. Instead, he was escaping the Carmichael Science and Medical Institute. He didn't think anything of it as he proceeded through the garage. As a car was leaving, he flagged it down, hoping to get a ride. The car stopped, and no one got out or said anything. Brodie walked to the driver's side window, and the driver slowly rolled the window down. He stared at the person as if he were looking at a ghost.

"Brodie," the woman said from the car. "Why are you out here?"

"Sheila," Brodie replied before passing out.

Chapter Thirteen

Present Day 2030

When Brodie came to, he was strapped down on a bed. There were no pictures on the walls nor furniture around the room. Right across from the bed was a two-way mirror. Brodie looked over at it, trying to see if he could see someone on the other side. He struggled to get loose, but he couldn't. He stared again at the two-way mirror.

"Whoever you are, just let me go! I don't know anything!" he shouted at the top of his lungs.

No one responded to his plea, which only made him madder. He knew someone was watching him on the other side of the mirror.

"You damn coward. Just kill me if you want me dead. You've already killed everybody I know." He struggled again to get loose.

While he pulled at the straps, the door next to the two-way mirror slowly opened. Brodie looked over at it, wondering who was entering. His eyes grew wider and wider as the door swung open, and when he saw Sheila and KJ enter the room, he almost had a heart attack. Sheila ran to his side to calm him down, and KJ placed an oxygen mask over his nose and mouth to help him breathe. It took a couple of minutes for Brodie to become calm enough to look at them, but he didn't speak a word. He was still processing this new reality. Sheila touched his arm and looked at him, but he didn't react. He thought it was all a dream.

"Brodie, are you okay?" she asked.

He didn't respond.

"Maybe he got brain damage or something," KJ said. "We don't know what the side effects might be."

"He said my name in the parking lot. I think he's alright. Just has to adjust to being back."

Brodie slit his eyes at her. "We buried you years ago."

"Something's not right, Sheila," KJ said with a forced smile. He looked at Brodie. "You sure you okay, boss?"

Brodie turned to face KJ. "You're dead, too."

KJ stared over at Sheila. "I hope that's not a side effect, that everyone you know is dead."

Brodie started to breathe heavily again. He grabbed the oxygen mask and took some deep breaths. "I don't get it. How can you guys be alive? Is this a dream?"

"No, Brodie, this is about as real as it gets. What year do you think it is?" KJ asked.

Brodie looked at both of them. "It's 2019."

They looked at each other with panic on their faces.

"KJ, let's talk in the other room," Sheila said as she walked to the door. KJ followed.

"Where are you guys going?" Brodie asked. "Let me out of these restraints."

Sheila and KJ ignored his request and walked out the door. When they got on the other side, they both took a deep breath trying to rationalize what had happened.

"This has never happened before," Sheila said.

"This is a major flaw, Sheila. He's the boss and came back to the wrong time period. He's going to shit his pants when we tell him he's eleven years off."

"I'm not sure what happened, but there has to be a reasonable explanation. And if he thinks we are both dead, he must know something about how we died. Let's go back in."

Sheila and KJ walk back into the room.

"Tell me what's going on," Brodie demanded. "I need answers."

Sheila began taking off the restraints as KJ looked on nervously. He wasn't too sure how Brodie would take all the news they were about to tell him.

"Okay, Brodie. It's actually 2030," Sheila said.

"What are you talking about? I was with Momma, Uncle Benny, and Cymone just yesterday."

Sheila took a deep breath herself. "Brodie, Momma died in 2015."

"No, you died in 2015," he replied. "Momma, Uncle Benny, and Cymone just died yesterday or a couple of days ago. I don't know how long I've been here."

"Momma is dead, but nobody has seen or talked to Uncle Benny in years. And who is this Cymone person? And how did they all die?"

165

Brodie was about to say more, but then he caught eyes with KJ. "I don't remember all the details of who killed them or why. I just know they were dead the last time I saw them."

"Who is Cymone?" KJ asked.

"She was the girl of my dreams. I loved her, but now she's dead."

KJ looked over at Sheila with a bugged-out look on his face. "You better not tell Sabrina that."

"Sabrina!" Brodie said with disgust on his lips.

"Your fiancée," said Sheila. "You two have been together since college. She's KJ's—"

Brodie finished Sheila's sentence for her. "Cousin. How did that happen? What happened with Alaina? I'm not with her?"

KJ laughed loudly. "Man, if you weren't my boy, I would tell my cousin you got a thing for her best friend and some girl named Cymone. You better remember soon; Sabrina don't like this crazy science shit."

"I didn't graduate from Purdue?"

"No, you never attended Purdue. You left Central State and went to Notre Dame. You wanted to, but you decided Notre Dame was better since you could live at home for free."

Brodie was confused. "But I never heard back from them. I didn't think they accepted me."

"Accepted you? Shit, they are about to name a building after you."

"So, I went to Notre Dame and lived at home by myself? Where were you at?" he asked Sheila, still confused.

"I moved out so that you could have your space. You and I wouldn't have survived under the same roof during that period of time." Sheila could tell her brother was struggling with understanding how things had come about. "You don't remember any of this?"

Brodie shrugged. "Until right now, I thought I went to Purdue."

"Maybe that's what happened this time around," KJ said, going back through his notebook. "In the past, you always went to Notre Dame. We always said you couldn't alter anything."

"Alter what? What's going on here?" Brodie asked, not understanding what either of them were alluding to.

"Brodie, you're one of the top physicists in the world. You invented time travel," Sheila said.

Brodie stared at both of them for a second and then laughed. "You two are crazy. There's no time travel. That shit ain't real."

"It wasn't until you made it happen. People laughed at you for years, but now everyone wants to be a part of your success." KJ patted him on the back. "We are about to change the world in a major way."

"So, if time travel is real, then maybe I was trying something new to see what would happen. Last thing I remember was Cymone dying in my arms. That was in Cleveland."

"Sheila, let's talk again," KJ said, walking quickly out the room. Sheila followed.

"You guys can include me in the discussion," Brodie said as the door closed. He rushed over to it and tried to open it himself, but it was locked on his side. "I'm sure you're discussing my life."

In the hallway, KJ said, "He altered everything. This Brodie didn't even go into science. He wasn't introduced to Sabrina by me, so he ended up with her best friend, Alaina, instead. But he also ran into some woman named Cymone. And don't let me forget, we all are dead."

Sheila sighed. "I know exactly what you are saying. The only option we have at this point and time is to have him go back again, but this time stick exactly to the script. I just hope this Brodie will listen and do that. We have a different Brodie than before. Damn!"

When they walked back in, Brodie was pacing the floor. "So, what happened from 2015 to 2030?" he asked.

"Where do you want me to start?" Sheila replied.

"Well, apparently, you didn't die, so let's start there."

"Okay, Momma and Daddy died in March of 2015. That fall, you transferred to Notre Dame…"

Brodie was shocked to hear that both his parents had died. He teared up. "How did they die?"

Sheila had a sad look on her face. "Home invasion. People came in to rob the place, but when Daddy woke up in the middle of the night, they killed them both."

"When did I die in this story?" KJ asked.

Brodie stared at him. "When did we become friends?"

"I helped you get a job here. And next thing I know, you were my boss, and then you quickly became everyone's boss. And eventually bought the building."

"I'm a scientist?" Brodie asked, shocked.

"Yeah, you are, little brother. You're quite famous, too."

Brodie shook his head in disbelief. "You got to be kidding me."

Sheila and KJ just looked at him with serious expressions on their faces.

"You are as famous as Jay-Z. Time travel has put you on the map," KJ said.

Brodie laughed loudly. "You two got to be joking with me. Time travel is not real. Are you saying I just got back from time traveling?"

Sheila smiled at KJ. "Everyone, even us, thought you were crazy. The past executives all got fired because you were right."

"But you always talk about it being possible," Brodie said to Sheila.

"Yeah, but you made it a reality," Sheila replied back to him.

"Prove it," Brodie said.

"You are the proof, Brodie," KJ said. "You have gone back several times now. But this is the first time that you didn't come all the way back to 2030."

"Has anyone else gone back?"

"Only you," Sheila said with confidence. "You didn't want anybody to suffer any side effects that you didn't suffer first. Next month, we do a demonstration for the President."

KJ was quiet on the subject of whether or not Brodie was the only one to time travel.

Brodie rubbed his bald head and looked at both of them. "I get the feeling that you two need me to go back in time again."

"Actually, we do. And it needs to happen as soon as possible," KJ said.

"I can go now," Brodie said with no thought of any other responsibilities he might have. "It's safe, right? I guess it has to be since I just came back."

"We can't today," Sheila said. "It's Sabrina's bachelorette party."

Brodie had a frown on his face. "And when are we getting married?"

"Next weekend. Brodie, I don't know what happened in the machine this last time, but in our present time, you and Sabrina are a really happy couple," Sheila said, trying to get her brother to not reject the thought of him being with Sabrina. "We'll have you go back on Sunday night."

KJ was upset that Brodie was dismissing his cousin. "But this time, Brodie, you have to stick with everything we say. We need you to go to Notre Dame and not Purdue. That decision alters everything. Remember, every different decision will affect all of us." KJ's cellphone rang. He looked at the number. "Hey, I need to make a run. I'll see you later. Sheila, make sure you give him a complete update on everything. We don't need this flaw leaking to the press."

He left the room.

"Definitely don't need our CEO not being able to remember that he's even our CEO." Sheila turned to Brodie. "Everything we have built depends on you going back and doing everything the right way."

"How many of these time machines do we have?"

"Two, but we haven't really tested the other one yet."

Brodie thought for a moment about his sister's response. "So, KJ could have gone back and altered things as well, which would cause me to alter things even more."

Sheila thought about what he'd just said. "I suppose he could have, but what does he have to gain? KJ is like family. Plus, you said he died."

"I didn't want to say it earlier, but KJ was working with a guy named Derek. KJ was involved in your death. I don't know how involved, but the trail led to him and then to Derek. Maybe somehow, I was on to them in 2030, and he went back and killed you instead while I was under."

"But that wouldn't make any sense."

"I agree. Why kill you?" Brodie asked.

"I did develop the basis for time travel. You just executed what I developed and took the credit." She smiled at him.

"Damn, that's cold of me."

"I'm not mad. You did take it to the next level. I couldn't have done it. I'm just glad you understood and saw what I was trying to say."

Brodie smiled. "Thanks. I don't want to be the greatest thief in history."

She winked at him. "It's alright. You haven't seen my paycheck."

Brodie sat on the edge of the bed. "Why did I go back in the first place?"

Sheila walked up to her brother. "You wanted to go back and stop Mom and Dad from being killed."

"Why couldn't I stop it?" He was perplexed that he hadn't been able to do it.

Sheila gently rubbed his back, comforting him. "I think that no matter what you tried, they still ended up dying."

"But not this last time, when you died. If Mom and Dad are meant to die on that day, then someone must have decided to kill you and get the time travel plans before you even shared them with me. My money is on KJ. Sorry, sis."

"I don't know. All I can say is that the research we are doing is very important. If you don't make things right, we are very screwed."

"Do you really trust KJ?"

"KJ is like family. You and him are thick as thieves. He loves you like a brother."

"Something just doesn't seem right. Is he a transgender?"

Sheila laughed. "KJ? No. He has a lot of girlfriends."

"I still don't trust him. You sure he doesn't wear dresses or makeup?"

Sheila rolled her eyes thinking he was just talking nonsense. "I really need you to go back in."

"Sheila, someone else has used these time machines before. Whoever it is, they didn't die."

Sheila thought about what he said for a couple of seconds and then laughed. "You think Sabrina went back?"

"Can't rule her out."

"You reaching brother. Sabrina can't operate an espresso machine without help. Definitely not her."

Chapter Fourteen

KJ sat down in the back of the restaurant, nervously looking at his phone. He stared around periodically, checking to see if anyone was eyeing him. Minutes later, a tall, dark figure came and sat down in front of him.

"What took you so long, Derek?" KJ said.

"Hey, I'm the one putting up all the money."

KJ exhaled. "But I'm taking all the risk."

"Okay, we both are important. What was the 911 text messages about?"

"What did you do, Derek?" KJ asked, staring him down. "I told you not to change a thing about the past."

"I didn't do anything but help him and Sabrina out."

"Bullshit! You've changed everything. You altered him."

"What do you mean?"

"Brodie went back in time, and this time around, his sister died, I died, and he never developed a time machine. Do you understand that if he had returned to 2030 like he was supposed to, then I would be dead right now? Once the person returns to the present date that they left, all that they changed occurs immediately once people awake after the return."

"Did I die?" Derek asked.

KJ thought about it. "I don't think so. He didn't mention it."

Derek scoffed. "Okay, yes, I had the sister killed. She's the brains behind the time machine. All I needed was her plans and to get her brother out the way. I didn't need him going to Notre Dame. He would have been very problematic for you."

"Somewhere everything got screwed up. His sister died, he went to Purdue, and I'm dead. Did you kill me?"

"Of course not. Did he mention me at all?" Derek asked.

"Surprisingly, no. He did mention some woman named Cymone."

Derek perked up. "Say that again?"

"Cymone. Do you know her?"

Derek had a serious look on his face. "What did he say about her?"

"That she was the love of his life. He was convinced she was real. But my sister and Alaina have never mentioned anyone by that name. Neither has he before."

"I don't think he told you everything," Derek said thinking hard about the situation.

"It won't matter now; he's going back in the machine tomorrow to correct everything."

Derek got nose to nose with KJ. "His sister and him need to die right after he goes back in."

"Why? Our business is still on track. After he marries my cousin, she will get half of the company. Then we can go in and change our financial status and live a comfortable life forever. Don't get greedy, Derek."

"So, did he have any side effects this time around?"

KJ smiled. "Nope. But you never answered me. Do you know this Cymone person?"

***

Sheila took Brodie to his mansion on the outskirts of the city. Upon entering his two hundred acres of land, he was amazed that he was living such a great life. Having a house fit for a king, where you needed to cross a moat, had been a fantasy of his as a child. Seeing that it had actually come true was unreal. With the tall gated wall and security guards, it was evident that he was a man of wealth and importance. He walked inside the house and gazed around like a kid at an amusement park.

"And this is my house," he said, standing in the foyer.

"Little brother, you made probably the biggest discovery in the history of mankind. This invention will change the lives of everyone."

Brodie smirked. "It will also make the greedy even greedier and the madmen of the world even worse. This might be the invention to end mankind, not help them."

Sheila looked at him. "So, what do you want to do? Whatever you decide, I'm with you."

As Brodie was about to speak, Sabrina came up from behind and hugged him. He turned around, shocked to see her. Before he could react, she jumped into his arms and kissed him. Brodie frowned, and Sabrina saw the look on his face.

"What's wrong, baby?" she asked, kissing him again. She looked over at Sheila to see if she knew what was bothering Brodie.

"I'm just tired," Brodie said as he pulled away from her. When he looked up, he saw Alaina coming down the long corridor to where they were waiting. He left Sheila and Sabrina and walked over to meet her. "Hey, Alaina." He smiled at her romantically. "How are you today?"

Alaina smiled back. "What have you been drinking today, Brodie?"

Sabrina turned him around to face her. "If I didn't know any better, I would think you and Alaina had something going on."

"I got a man," Alaina said.

"Brodie's not smart enough to pull that off," Sheila said, stepping in to help her brother out.

"It is funny. I didn't think I was one of your favorite people," Alaina said, looking at him sideways.

Brodie stared at Alaina. "I'm sorry if I ever made you feel that way. What are you ladies doing today, anyway?"

Sabrina looked at him like he was crazy. "Bachelorette party. Remember?"

"Oh, got it. It's here," Brodie said as though he had forgotten it.

"Something is definitely off with you, Brodie. I haven't figured it out yet, but I'm getting there," Sabrina said, staring him in the eyes.

"So, where is the wedding dress?" Sheila asked, hoping to change the subject.

The wedding dress comment brought a joyous smile to Sabrina's face. She was looking forward to becoming Brodie's wife.

"I thought I showed you already. It's upstairs," she said, smiling from ear to ear. "Come on, I'll show you."

Sheila got a thought in her head. "Brodie, I need to talk to you."

"Go ahead," he said, looking at the other women in the room.

"It's about work. I don't want to bore them."

Alaina rolled her eyes. "Time travel talk. Definitely not my cup of tea. Let's go see the dress."

"I'll be right up," Sheila said as Alaina and Sabrina started walking up the stairs.

Sheila grabbed Brodie, and they went back outside to the driveway.

"What's the big urgency?" he asked.

"You're telling me I'm dead."

"But you're alive," Brodie said, not understanding where his sister was going with the conversation.

"I'm only alive because you haven't come back to 2030. If you had come back, I'm not sure what would have happened. With everyone dead, there would be only one person able to be there when you returned."

"Who is that?"

"Your fiancée, Sabrina."

"Sabrina! I thought you said she couldn't operate an espresso machine."

"I know, but it's the only plausible answer and with everyone out of the way, she wins."

"Makes sense to me."

"But if you go back in and come back to 2030 based on your new reality of not being a scientist then time travel is over. You won't ever be able to go back and change anything."

"What happens when I go to sleep tonight? Do I wake up in this reality of 2019, or do I fast forward to 2030, and you're dead? I think I need to go back in time tonight."

Sheila didn't know for sure what would happen if Brodie went to sleep. The thought scared her knowing that his sleep could mean her permanent death. "I think you're right. It has to be right after the party."

Brodie gave her a serious look. "You can't tell KJ."

"Why not?"

"I'm telling you he's working with this guy named Derek and they are trying to get their hands on the time machine. When I go back in time, shut down the other machine until I get back. I don't need to see someone trying to kill me in the past. Not again."

"Okay, but I think you're wrong about KJ."

"I think I'm right. I think they killed you to get the time machine plans you had started on. But when they couldn't find them, they figured that there was only one person you trusted with your life like that and that was me."

Sheila nodded in agreement.

"I think KJ and some other people have been going back as well altering and creating different timelines. I think that's why you keep dying because they want the original plans."

"That's not going to happen. We're going to stop them this time around."

Brodie seemed confident. "I think I can save everyone."

Sheila exhaled. "Brodie, this isn't a lifesaving mission. Our lives, our universe, and our careers are at stake. Just go back and make things right. I will write everything down for you. You can't mess this up."

"What about Cymone?" Brodie asked with love in his eyes.

Sheila shook her head at him. "Please forget about this Cymone person."

***

That afternoon, Brodie walked around his house, making sure no one was home. When he reached his library, he closed the door and turned on the computer at his desk. He input "Cymone Cartwright" in the search bar. He saw that her current address was in Oakland, California. He then paid for the deeper search that would provide him her actual address and a phone number. He hesitated for a few minutes before dialing it.

"Hello," Cymone said on her end.

Brodie was shocked. He didn't really know how to start the conversation, so he stayed quiet. It felt good just to hear her voice.

"Okay, creep, I hear you breathing," she said, annoyed by the silence.

"Hey, Cymone."

"Who is this?" she asked.

Brodie took a deep breath. "This is really going to sound weird, but we met before…"

"What's your name?"

"Brodie Carmichael."

Cymone went silent for a moment. "I don't know any Brodie. Sorry, dude, you got the wrong number. And definitely the wrong Cymone."

"Please don't hang up. I know it sounds crazy, but I have met you. You are the right Cymone."

"Sorry, bye." Cymone hung up.

Brodie quickly redialed the number three more times until she finally picked up again.

"Derek, quit playing around on the phone," she said.

"I'm not Derek. You shouldn't trust him either," Brodie said, angry at the fact that she was with Derek.

"I'm going to block your number. Quit calling me!"

"I dropped my wallet, you picked it up, and that's when we met. Your favorite movie is *Boomerang*. You used to date a guy named Raymond."

Cymone went silent for several moments. Finally, she said. "How do you know that? That's how I met Derek, not you."

"I'm telling you the truth. I know you. I know this all seems out-of-this-world crazy, but I'm a time traveler."

"Bye," she said. "You weirdo."

"No, I'm not weird. It's the truth. You're from Detroit, but your grandmother is from Ohio. Your mother and grandmother can't live in the same city or state. Your favorite song is 'If Only for One Night' by Luther Vandross."

"Shit! I got to go." Cymone hung up the phone in haste. She stared at it like it was going to attack her. "How does he know that?" she asked herself.

Brodie called back several times, but she never picked up the phone again. She thought about blocking his number but then decided against it. Though it scared her, she was curious as to how he knew the things he did. Especially since she hadn't told anybody that about her favorite song; even Derek didn't know about that one. To clear her head, she left the phone on the table and took a walk outside.

While Cymone went to calm her nerves, Brodie sat at his desk and hopelessly cried. "I don't want to let you go."

As Cymone wandered down her street, she couldn't help but think that maybe there was some truth to what he had said to her.

"What if," she said to herself as a car pulled up to the curb. The black-tinted windows rolled down.

"Hey, babe, are you okay?" Derek asked with a big smile on his face.

Cymone stared at him. "Derek, do you know a guy named Brodie?"

Derek froze, and his smile disappeared as he thought of what to say.

"Do you know the guy or not?" she asked again.

"What did he want?"

"You know him?"

"No, but by the look on your face, it seems like he upset you."

She accepted his answer, but she wasn't a hundred percent sure she trusted it. "I'll see you when I get back from my walk," she said, stepping away from his car.

"What did he want?" Derek asked. He knew there was information that she was keeping from him.

"I don't know. I hung up on him after he told me he knew what my favorite song was," Cymone said, her eyes stuck on Derek.

"What did he say was your favorite song?" Derek asked, trying to dig deeper into what Brodie might have mentioned to her.

"What do you think? You know it, right?"

Derek was at a loss. His brain scrambled to figure out what it might be. He had no clue, so he took a big guess. "That's easy," he said, faking a smile. "That one Beyoncé song about girl power."

Cymone smiled. "Yeah, that's exactly what he said as well."

"Get in the car. I'll give you a lift back to the house. I got a surprise for you tonight."

She grinned. "That's so sweet. I think I'm going to keep walking for a bit."

"Okay, don't say I didn't offer."

"Derek, I'll see you when I get back," she said as she started walking again.

As she headed down the street, Derek fumed. He quickly picked up his cell phone and dialed a number.

KJ picked up on the other end. "Hello," he said.

"He called her," Derek said with a tone filled with meanness. "He has to die."

"He called who? What are you even talking about, man? Who is he?" KJ replied, a little annoyed at how Derek was talking to him.

"Brodie called Cymone."

"I thought you said you didn't know a Cymone."

"That's beside the point. I can't have him ruin what Cymone and I have."

KJ was pissed. "You and my sister can kiss my ass. I have gone above and beyond to make you guys happy. I need him to go back and correct the bullshit you did the last time you went back. You fuckin' killed me."

"Don't believe them lies he told you. We are partners. I got your back. Let's go in the time machine together and make this right for us."

"We can't go back together. There'll be nobody there to open the portal for our return. We can take off together, but someone always has to be waiting in the room on the return."

"I can go back," Derek said, like that was the answer to all their problems.

"Hell no. I'm going back. And I will make this the way it's supposed to be. You will get your precious Cymone, and we will own the market on time travel," KJ said with a huff. "And Sabrina will get her Brodie."

"I'll fly back there tonight," Derek said. "I want to be there."

"Nope. This trip will be just me going in and my sister waiting for my return."

"You don't trust me?"

KJ exhaled. "Frankly, no. Bye, Derek." KJ hung up.

***

Later that night, Sheila slipped out of the bachelorette party. Her departure was unnoticed by everyone except for Sabrina. As Sheila jumped in her car and headed back to the office building, she didn't notice that someone was following her.

At the lab, Brodie waited. To pass the time, he looked at the pictures in his wallet of him and Sabrina. They seemed so happy.

"Why do I hate her so much when I went to Purdue? It doesn't make any sense," he said to himself. "Go to Notre Dame, she's the love of my life. Go to Purdue, she's my sworn enemy. Damn, sliding doors." He looked around the lab. "I really screwed up going to Purdue. I have no clue how any of this shit works. I love you, Cymone. How can we meet again if not at Purdue?" He scratched his head in frustration.

When Sheila pulled into the parking garage and got out of her car, she carefully looked around to see if she had been followed. She didn't see anyone. As she entered the building, a dark shadow appeared from one of the pillars near where she'd parked.

The moment she walked into the lab, she noticed that Brodie had fallen asleep in the time machine capsule. She quickly strode over to him and gave him a shove.

"What are you doing? Trying to kill me?"

Brodie woke up, flushed. "I'm sorry. I got bored."

She shook her head. "Damn, I don't know what you did with old Brodie. He loved being in this lab. That's all he lived for."

"Maybe that's why I changed things, to see how my life would have gone if I made a different choice."

"I always thought you were happy doing the work we do."

Brodie frowned. He wanted to tell her something, but he resisted. "This all seems foreign to me."

"You didn't contact this Cymone or Derek, did you?" Sheila asked, expecting the answer to be yes.

"No," Brodie said, lying to her. "I thought about it, but then I figured she wouldn't believe me."

"Thank God you didn't. You have to remember she was a mistake."

"She's the best mistake I have ever made."

"What do you want, Brodie?" Sheila threw up her hands.

"I don't know. She's the best part of my memories."

"You have a choice to make. I can set the time machine for you to come to 2030, or you can go back to 2015. Just remember, if you go to 2030, I won't be here, Cymone won't be here, Uncle Benny, Momma, and even KJ won't be here when you get back. It'll be just you, Alaina, and Sabrina. Even the time machine will disappear because you didn't invent it."

"I get it. 2015." Brodie shook his head as he felt the weight of the world on his shoulders. "I have no clue how any of this works," he said, shamefully embarrassed by his lack of knowledge of the lab.

"It's okay. Once you go back in and change things back to the way they are supposed to be, we should put an end to this time travel stuff. You are right, somebody will use this for evil. Just imagine someone going back and helping Hitler win World War II. Or even worse than that, have the Confederates win the Civil War. Who knows how long slavery would have lasted under them? Time machines give people too much power."

"Agreed. When are you going to shut down the other time machine?" Brodie asked.

"Right after you go back in. I'm making a note for myself too. I won't be the same person either. I'll secure everything and make sure that the other one will not work again in my lifetime." She smiled. "If I'm still alive, of course."

"Let's do this," Brodie said, pumping himself up. "I'll make it all right again."

Sheila handed him some pills. They were the same ones from when he was in his dorm room back at Central State. "Take these. They will make you relax."

Brodie looked at her. "Did you give me these anytime back in 2015?"

"No, why?"

"I remember taking these pills that night before finding out that you were killed."

"We didn't start using these pills until this year. Are you sure these are the same pills?" Sheila was now really concerned about him going back. She didn't say it, but she was beginning to believe that maybe he was right about KJ.

"Is that a problem?"

"It shouldn't be," Sheila said trying to convey confidence.

"Why did you say it like that?" he asked with a concerned, almost scared look on his face. "KJ went back before?"

"I hope not. But it wouldn't make any sense that he would let himself die. Sabrina was really hurt when he died."

"So, she couldn't have been working against KJ."

"You got a point there. KJ would have to be the biggest idiot alive to do that. Unless the person he's working with double-crossed him. Just tell me how all this works."

Sheila took a deep breath. "Okay, after you take these pills, you're going to get very sleepy. There's a jolt when the machine spins. When you get back to 2015, it's going to be that same day. No matter what, do not take these pills again. I have the settings on the time machine to go from 2015 to 2030 today. You will have approximately six hours in real time. You need to make sure that you go to Notre Dame. Also, even if I'm dead, you need to make sure you get the files that I created for the time travel machine." She handed him something that looked like a remote. "This here will be your abort remote. Push the red button, and it will bring you back to 2030. You will automatically be brought back to 2030 in 6 hours no matter what. Just don't screw up things, Brodie. And if you see anything out of the ordinary, you have to eliminate it—or them."

"I have to kill someone?" Brodie asked, not really wanting to do that.

"It's either us or them at this point." Sheila gave him a backpack. "Inside the bag is a gun, rope, tape, and a medical kit. Just need to be prepared for anything even running into Young Brodie, which you need to save his life. If he dies, it doesn't matter what button you push, you not coming back to the future."

"You're starting to scare me now."

"I just think you might be right about KJ. He didn't say anything today when you asked if anyone else had gone back in time. I remember now that last week, he had some visitors in here, but he didn't have them sign in."

"How come you can't come with me?" Brodie asked as fear spread across his face.

"We can't afford for the both of us to be stuck in time. I have to make sure you go back and return on this date in 2030. When you return, your body goes through a lot of changes. It's scary because it's almost like you're in a coma. I can't go to sleep the whole time you're gone because if I did, I would forget everything that we are doing right now. Once I go to sleep, I wake up in the new world you have changed. And my memory of this moment doesn't exist anymore."

"Damn, has this happened every time I've come back?"

Sheila looked away. Seeing the fear on Brodie's face, she really didn't want to answer that question. "Yeah. This last time was the worst, though."

"Damn!"

"Just do what I told you, and we should be fine. If you do run into KJ, you need to kill him before he kills you or me. He probably knows by now that we are on to him. He's been secretive all day. Hasn't returned any of my calls."

"I knew it. KJ is a crook."

Sheila handed him a note with instructions. "Give this to the younger you. He needs to follow the directions for his life and ours."

"I got it," Brodie said, understanding the point she was making.

Sheila looked at him, waiting for him. Finally, she said, "You need to take the pills first, little brother."

Brodie chuckled. "Oh yeah, right." He threw the pills in his mouth and followed them with a gulp of water from a glass that Sheila handed him. "Done."

"This is going to be quick. Count backwards from twenty."

"Twenty, nineteen, eighteen, seventeen, sixteen, fifteen, fourteen…"

Brodie was knocked out at fourteen. Sheila closed the time capsule and locked it. She then turned on the machine and pressed the date back to March 11, 2015.

"I hope that gives you enough time to do what I know you want to do, little brother."

Sheila said a silent prayer and pushed the green button to send her brother back in time. She grabbed his cell phone and put it in her lab coat. After Brodie disappeared, she saw a shadow down the hallway head into the other room, where the second time machine was. Sheila finished up what she was doing. When she entered the hallway, she tried to turn on the lights, but they didn't come on. She locked the door to the lab Brodie had just left from. Then she slowly walked down the dark hallway to shut down the other time machine. When she got to the room, the door was locked. Through a window in the door, she saw Sabrina helping KJ operate the other time travel machine. She beat on the door for them to stop, but they ignored her.

"KJ, don't do it! You're going to kill me or Brodie!"

After KJ fell asleep, Sabrina followed the same procedure that Sheila had done to send Brodie back in time. After she closed the capsule and pushed the green button, she sat down in a chair and just stared at Sheila.

"Why are you doing this, Sabrina?"

"I want to be happy, too. If I can't have Brodie, then nobody will."

"No! No! No! You and Brodie will be together. That's the reality we know now."

"You don't understand, Sheila. It took me and KJ so many times to get Brodie to be my man, my husband. I love him."

"In 2030, he loves you, nobody else."

Sabrina rolled her eyes. "You just don't understand."

"You decided to kill me?" Sheila asked, wanting to break the door down and strangle Sabrina. She remembered the door control panel and looked over at it.

"You dying was what we thought would make everyone happy, but that damn Brodie just had to screw things up and decide to go to Purdue this last time to see how his life would have turned out. We had it all figured out. I got Brodie, KJ got the time machine, and we all got rich."

"Brodie loves you."

Sabrina laughed. "Brodie loves Cymone or Alaina. I've lost track. He will love me this time around."

"You won't win, Sabrina."

Sabrina raised up and looked desperately at Sheila. She knew Sheila had something up her sleeve. She pointed at her. "I got you."

"What?" Sheila asked, not clear on what Sabrina was referring to.

Sabrina put a time on the time machine and got in the same chair that KJ had.

Sheila saw what she was planning to do. "No, Sabrina, you're going to kill yourself and KJ!" she yelled. Sheila raced to the door control panel and pressed in the code to override the code that Sabrina had used to lock the door.

Sabrina pushed the green button and quickly closed the hatch on the time machine. Sheila looked on as the clock counted down from twenty, and then Sabrina disappeared into thin air like the others as Sheila struggled to get the door to open.

Chapter Fifteen

Brodie appeared out of thin air behind the school library on the campus of Central State University. He quickly looked at his watch and saw that the date was March 11, 2015, and the time was 5:30 p.m.

"Thank you, Sheila." He knew the change in date was her idea to give him time to figure out what to do. "Okay, Brodie, you can do this," he said to himself. His eyes wandered over the campus yard, and he saw the younger version of himself strolling along right past him without even noticing that the Older Brodie was even there. "You were so innocent then."

Out of nowhere, he saw Older KJ appear on the other side of the yard.

"Shit, I knew he was using the other time machine. Sheila is too trusting," Brodie said.

Older KJ looked over at him and then at the younger Brodie. He pulled out a gun and started to walk toward the younger Brodie. When the older Brodie saw what KJ was trying to do, he immediately ran down the younger Brodie and grabbed him, and the younger Brodie finally saw the resemblance.

"Do I know you?" the younger Brodie asked with his fist up.

"That guy over there is about to kill you. We need to get you to a safe place."

"Who?" the younger Brodie asked. Then he looked over and saw KJ running towards them with his gun in hand. "This way," he said as he and the older Brodie ran into the dorm.

They ran up five flights of stairs and then up another half flight to a crawlspace just large enough for two people to hide. The younger Brodie jumped in and made room for the older Brodie.

"Get in," he insisted.

"I got to go somewhere else, but you lock this door, and no matter what, do not open it for at least six hours. If this guy kills you, he will alter everything."

"Alter what? Why is he trying to kill me?"

"You wouldn't believe me if I told you."

The younger Brodie smirked. "Is this a frat prank? Mad because I didn't join?"

The older Brodie grabbed the younger version of himself by the arms and looked deep into his eyes. "This is no joke. You cannot come out and risk getting shot by this guy. Please believe me. Your future depends on you staying here and alive."

"Then why don't you stay with me?"

"I have to go and try and save Sheila and your mother and father."

"Who are these people?" the younger Brodie asked, growing increasingly scared.

"Check this out. If you stay in here for six hours and don't say a word no matter who is on the other side, I will come back and explain it all to you. But I have to go to South Bend now."

"Really?"

"Do what I say, and everything will turn out fine," the older Brodie said, knowing that in six hours, he would hopefully be back in the year 2030. He also handed the younger Brodie a note, which the younger Brodie quickly read.

"You want me to go to Notre Dame next year for school?"

"Yeah, it's very important that you do."

"I don't play football, so hopefully, this isn't some recruitment ploy," the younger Brodie said.

"No. You have to do these things. Promise me," the older Brodie begged. In his mind, he couldn't believe how stubborn the younger Brodie was.

"Okay, but you also want me to go to Purdue next summer for summer school to meet this girl Cymone on the first day of summer school? Is this necessary?"

"She's the one. Don't mess this up."

They heard KJ's footsteps coming up the stairs. Older Brodie instructed the younger Brodie to be silent, and then he quietly helped him close the door. As the younger Brodie locked it from his side, the older Brodie escaped down the fire escape. Meanwhile, KJ still searched the building, trying to find them both.

When Brodie got to the street, he saw one of the college students at the credit union getting cash out of the ATM. He noticed that they had left their car running, so he rushed over to it, got inside, and drove off.

***

In the year 2025, Sabrina appeared in the women's restroom at the Carmichael Science and Medical Institute. She looked in the mirror to gather herself. In the past, either KJ or Derek had mostly gone in the second time machine, but rarely her. She was typically the person who stayed back. Her confidence seemed to be growing, but then Sheila walked into the restroom. Sabrina panicked and began to sweat.

"I'm not going to lose Brodie," Sabrina said.

Sheila gave her a strange look. "Going to lose Brodie? You okay, girl?"

Sabrina sensed that this was not the same Sheila she had just left in the lab. "Where is Brodie?"

"Sabrina, you are acting really weird. I thought you went to lunch with KJ?" Sheila looked her up and down.

"I forgot something," Sabrina replied back nervously.

Sheila huffed. "And weren't you wearing a red dress? I do like that outfit you got on."

"Where is Brodie?" Sabrina asked again.

"You act like you weren't at their house last night for the party celebrating our breakthrough."

"Yeah, but I thought I had a meeting with him."

"Girl, Brodie and Cymone are in Las Vegas. He said he didn't want to be disturbed," Sheila said with authority. "I'm surprised your bestie Cymone didn't text you this morning. But if it's an emergency, I'm sure his admin, Barbara, will get you in contact with him."

"Damn, really? She's my best friend?" Sabrina said as she abruptly left the restroom. When she got to the hallway, she was mad as hell. "I'm that bitch's friend." She then looked over and saw Barbara filing her nails.

***

About ten minutes later, Sheila went to get some water from the office breakroom kitchen. She noticed Sabrina and KJ come in. She also noticed that Sabrina now had on a red dress.

"Something isn't right," she said to herself trying to figure things out in her head.

***

Passing by the "Welcome to South Bend" sign, Brodie exhaled in jubilation. So far, he felt things were going well. The fact that he was still alive meant that KJ hadn't gotten to the younger Brodie yet nor made it back to 2030. He raced down US 31 to the southeast side of town. Then he turned right on Indiana Avenue and headed down it until he reached his parent's house three blocks down. He stopped the car, jumped out, and ran into his parents' house. Both of his parents were sitting on the couch, watching *Jeopardy*, when he burst in.

"What are you doing here, Brodie?" his mother asked, while his father gave him the side-eye. "You look older. Are you stressed at school like that?"

"Mom, I'm not stressed out. I'm healthy and fine," Brodie said with a smile.

His mother and father looked at each other curious about his new appearance.

Brodie grew impatient. "I just need to get you two out of here now. It's not safe."

"What you do now?" his father asked as he sat up on the couch. "I'm not bailing you out of jail."

"Nobody's going to jail," Brodie said, holding back from yelling at his father for making the accusation. "People are trying to kill us."

"I'm not going nowhere. This boy has lost it," his father said as he turned his attention back to the game show.

Brodie grabbed the remote and turned off the TV. "For once in your life, just listen to me and go. I have already booked a hotel for you guys in Chicago. If you get on the road now, we should all be safe."

Gloria got up from the couch and looked him in the eye. "Are you really serious, Brodie?"

"Momma, I'm not playing around with you. We need to be out of this house for at least the next …" He looked at his watch. "… three and a half hours."

His mother turned to his father. "He's serious, Paul, let's go."

"Thank you," Brodie said as his father turned up his lips at him.

"Do we need to pack anything?" Gloria asked.

"No, just go to Chicago and spend the night. In the morning, everything should be just fine. But we need to leave right now." Brodie waved his hands, urging his parents to hurry up.

"Get the keys, Paul!" Gloria shouted.

"Where is Sheila at?" Brodie asked.

Paul grabbed the car keys and walked outside.

"She just went to the store down the street," Gloria said.

"How long ago?" Brodie asked.

"Five minutes ago."

"Get in the car now. I'll get Sheila, and she'll meet you guys there." He handed his mother a piece of paper. "This is the hotel name and address." He helped his mother into the car. "Straight to Chicago," he said, and then his father drove away.

After his parents had left, Brodie ran down the street to the corner store. When he got inside, he saw his sister in the dairy section. He also scoped the store to see if anybody was there aside from him, her, and the store clerk. He saw no one. He slowly walked over to his sister.

"Sheila," he said from behind her.

She turned around and jumped. Everything that she had in her hands fell to the floor. "Shoot! Brodie, what are you doing here?" She grabbed her mouth to hold back from screaming. Her eyes bulged out in amazement.

"I…"

Sheila yelled. She couldn't control herself. "It worked. Oh my God, it actually worked. Damn, you look older."

"You know?" Brodie asked, wondering what she was talking about.

"I never believed that time travel would be taken seriously. People always laughed at me. What year are you from?"

"2030."

"Fifteen years from now. You look pretty good for your age, bro. What about me? Am I married? Do I have kids? So many questions I have."

"I can't tell you," he said, slightly looking away.

She could tell something was wrong. "Why are you here?"

Brodie sighed. "I came to save you."

"From what?"

"KJ is coming to kill you."

Sheila laughed loudly. "You got to be joking. I just met KJ. He seems like cool people, not a killer." She paused and then realized what was happening. "He killed me already?"

Brodie nodded. "I came back to save you, Mom, and Dad. I just sent them to Chicago. The KJ from my time wants us dead."

Sheila exhaled. "Where have you been so far? Have you seen the 2030 KJ here?"

"Yeah, he was chasing me and my younger self around Central State's campus."

"Where is the younger you at now?" Sheila asked with a concerned look on her face.

"He's safe. If KJ had gotten to him, I wouldn't be here right now. KJ needs me dead more than anything. I figure he's on his way here to find me and probably kill us all."

"What are we doing? We have to kill KJ."

Brodie let out a light chuckle. "That's what 2030 Sheila told me as well."

"So, I am alive in 2030?" she asked with a smile on her face.

"Not really. I went back to 2015 before today and made some changes. KJ and this guy named Derek made some changes. You died, I went to Purdue, and the time machine never existed."

"Whoa!"

"Yeah, I saw a lot this last time."

She noticed the hesitation on his face. "A lot of people must have died."

"But not this time," Brodie said with optimism. "I'm getting you to safety."

"Let's go to Chicago," Sheila said, and she headed to the store's exit.

They jumped in her car and took off. As they were making a right turn, 2030 KJ was parking his car in front of the store.

***

Back in 2025, it was late in the evening by the time Sabrina got off the company's other jet at McCarren Airport in Las Vegas. She looked at her watch with irritation, and she fumed as she stepped into the limo. "I got one hour. Driver, take me to the Wynn."

***

Brodie and Sheila arrived at the hotel in Chicago. They were both puzzled when the reception clerk told them that their parents hadn't checked in yet. Sheila called her mother's phone, but Gloria didn't pick up.

"You don't think—"

"That our father would have them go back?" Brodie said, finishing the sentence.

He looked at his watch. "There's nothing I can do at this point. I have thirty minutes before going back to 2030. There's no way we can make it to South Bend. I'm calling the police. Hopefully, they can go to the house and check things out."

***

As Brodie expected, his parents went back home. Judging from their faces and the fact that they were not speaking to each other, one could tell that the ride back had been filled with arguments. As Brodie's father, Paul, parked the car in the driveway, the couple's attention was drawn to the light in the bathroom.

"I thought you cut off all the lights," Paul said.

"You need to stop talking to me right now. Our son asked us to do one thing, and you couldn't even do that. I should have gotten out the car on the toll road."

Paul looked around. "That boy was talking nonsense. Do you see anybody around here about to kill us? Please. I should have hit him across the head, talking that crazy shit. Why do you even pay for him to go to college?"

Gloria huffed and stomped into the house. Paul followed nonchalantly. When Gloria came to an abrupt stop, he ran into her backside.

"What's wrong with you?" he said.

Gloria's eyes shifted to the couch. Sitting there with his gun pointed at them was the older KJ. "Man, Brodie always said his father was the biggest hardheaded and stubborn man he ever knew. Damn, was he right. I got to give it up to Brodie; his plan almost came off flawlessly. If it wasn't for you two turning around, it would have worked."

Gloria turned to look at her husband. She had nothing but hatred for him at that point.

"What do you want from us? Does Brodie owe you money?" Paul asked thinking that was the answer.

KJ laughed. "You think this is about money? No, believe it or not, your son actually invented time travel. Quite a success, I might say. I figured I should at least let you know that he wasn't a failure in life. A genius according to several magazines and journals. He even won a Nobel Peace Prize."

"See, he's on those drugs, too," Paul said to Gloria.

"Drugs? No, sir, no drugs in my system. Just telling you the truth. And in twenty minutes, I will be back in the year 2030, but you won't know, because you'll be dead."

"I'll kill you," Paul said, stomping toward KJ.

Without hesitation, KJ shot Paul and then shot Gloria. He got up and walked out of the house like nothing had happened.

***

Back in 2025, upon arriving at the Wynn Hotel, Sabrina immediately saw Brodie at the blackjack table. She went over to him and hugged him from behind.

"Hey, Brodie," she said with a big smile on her face.

He turned and was shocked to see her. "Sabrina, why are you out here?"

"Well, I felt I needed a break, too. So, I jumped on the jet and came right here to see my two best friends in the world."

Brodie laughed. "You must be drinking. You know you hate me."

"Never. Hate is such a bad word. Let's drink to forgiveness. What are you drinking?"

Brodie shrugged. "Okay. Rum and Coke."

"I'll be right back."

Sabrina went to the bar and had the bartender make two rum and Cokes. After the drinks were made, she put something in Brodie's drink.

"No more time travel for you without me," she said to herself as she took the drinks back to where Brodie was playing blackjack. She handed him his drink. "To you and me being best friends." She held her glass up to toast.

Brodie obliged and tapped glasses with her. "I second that."

"Where is my bestie anyway?" Sabrina asked, looking around the casino.

"Still in the room getting dressed. You should go up there and surprise her." Brodie took out his room key and gave it to her.

"Are you sure?" she asked devilishly. "Because I am going to surprise her."

"She will love the surprise." Brodie reached in his pocket and pulled out a ring box. "Before you go, check this out." He opened it, and the diamond ring inside was blinding.

Sabrina fumed. "You bought that for her?" she asked with a little bit of attitude. She was upset that the ring he'd gotten her was substantially smaller than this one.

"You don't like it?"

She cleared the lump of hatred she had in her throat. "It's beautiful."

"Thanks," Brodie said, smiling. "I'm in love with this woman."

"She will love it. By the way, the restroom is over there." Sabrina pointed to where the restrooms were located.

"I don't have to go right now."

"Take care, Brodie," she said and then she walked over to the elevators. She looked at her watch. "Yeah, Cymone, I'm coming for you, bitch."

***

Back in 2015, as time to save his parents were disappearing, Brodie and Sheila were both trying to call their parents, but neither got a response. Brodie checked his watch. He shook his head in distress fearing the worst had happened.

"Damn, I only have five minutes left."

Sheila finally got their next-door neighbor, Mrs. Marshall, on the phone. "Mrs. Marshall, thank God you answered."

Mrs. Marshall could hear the desperation in Sheila's voice. "Are you okay, baby?"

"Can you do me a favor?" Sheila asked.

"Anything."

"Please go check on my parents. We have been calling them for almost an hour, but no one is answering the phone."

Mrs. Marshall walked over to her window and looked out. She saw their parents' car in the driveway. "They are home. I see their car in the driveway. Give me a minute, and I will go knock on the door. Probably watching the eleven o'clock news. Hold on. I see your brother getting out of a car."

"My brother?" Sheila asked looking over at Brodie.

Brodie was in disbelief that his younger self didn't listen.

"Yeah, Brodie. I'll go in with him. Hold on," Mrs. Marshall said.

Older Brodie screamed from the background, "He can't be there!" He looked over at his sister nervously. "We only have three minutes left. If he dies, then I die. And…" Brodie stopped talking.

One look in his eyes, Sheila figured it out. "I die also, right?"

"Why didn't he just listen?" Brodie asked out loud.

"Mrs. Marshall, please tell Brodie to come to you. Yell it to him," Sheila pleaded.

"Okay." Mrs. Marshall opened up the window and yelled, "Brodie! Brodie! Brodie!"

On the third time, she finally got his attention, right before he was about to enter the house. He waved at her.

"Hey, Mrs. Marshall."

"Brodie, come here. Your sister wants to talk to you. She's on the phone." She showed him the phone.

The younger Brodie changed his course and walked toward Mrs. Marshall's house. As he reached her door, Older KJ got out of his car.

***

Back in 2030, Sheila got the door open and looked at the control board and saw the date 2025. "Why is she going back to 2025?" Sheila asked herself.

Sheila's head dropped in pain. Then she felt a vibration in her lab jacket. She stared at the phone number before answering it.

"Hello."

"Hi, my name is Cymone, and a man named—"

"Brodie called you," Sheila said, completing her sentence. "I knew it," she said to herself.

"Do we know each other?" Cymone asked, still confused by it all.

"No."

"Brodie said he knows me. He knows some things about me that no one knows. I just don't know how it's possible. He even told me not to trust my husband, Derek."

Sheila's eyes popped. "You shouldn't."

"Hey babe, I didn't know you were back already," Derek said in the background.

Cymone got quiet.

"Derek is a killer," Sheila said whispering into the phone. "Be careful."

Cymone looked over at Derek strangely. "Are you sure?" she asked Sheila. "That's impossible."

"I would bet my life on it. You are in danger."

"Who are you talking to?" Derek asked as he moved closer to Cymone.

Cymone hung up the phone. "No one. Just a spam caller."

"And you answered it?" Derek asked looking at her believing she wasn't telling him the truth.

Sheila hung up the phone on her end and commenced to terminating time machine two from commission. To ensure it wouldn't work again, she smashed the system control panel with a hammer she found in the storage closet.

***

Back in 2015, Older KJ called out to Young Brodie. "Hey, Brodie, she's lying to you. I know where your sister is at. I can take you to her. She's safe," Older KJ said with a crooked smile.

"Who are you?" Young Brodie asked, trying to remember where he knew Older KJ from.

"I'm your sister's friend. We work together."

Young Brodie froze as he finally recognized Older KJ as the person who had tried to kill him on campus. Older KJ saw Young Brodie's hesitation and pulled out his gun.

"Oh Lord, this man has a gun," Mrs. Marshall said into the phone.

A policeman in his patrol car saw Older KJ with the gun. He called for backup, and then he and his partner jumped out of the car and ran down the street. They split up, approaching Older KJ on each side.

"Put the gun down, sir," said the officer who had been driving the car.

Older KJ ignored them and started shooting at Young Brodie. Young Brodie dropped to the ground and scurried around a car to hide behind it. The officers fired at Older KJ.

Older KJ ducked behind a car and looked at his watch. "I'll be out of here soon," he said with a chuckle. He pulled out his remote and pushed the exit button to return to present day, but nothing happened.

***

With Cymone tied up and hanging from the chandelier, Sabrina, who was sitting on the bed, marveled at the predicament Cymone was now in. While Cymone did everything possible to stay on her tippy-toes, Sabrina searched the internet for shoes.

"Why are you doing this, Sabrina? I thought we were friends!"

"I hate you. You have to die," Sabrina said with a smile. "I'm tired of you living my world. You know I have killed you in this room before, but Brodie still ended up with someone else. Tonight, I change all that."

"What are you talking about? Is this about Brodie? You hate him."

Sabrina abruptly stood up and rushed to Cymone. She slowly began to move the chair away from Cymone's feet. Cymone struggled to stay balanced. With her hands tied behind her back, there was nothing for her to grab on. Her eyes bulged as she realized she couldn't escape and that her screams and begging meant nothing to anyone. She braced herself for the chair being snatched away. Her body became tense, like a stone, and she feared the end was imminent.

As her toes neared the end of the chair seat, she let out one final scream. "I'm sorry. I never meant to hurt you. Please don't do this," she begged. "Sabrina, this isn't right."

"Only time will tell if it's wrong."

Without any hesitation, Sabrina pulled the chair away. Cymone began struggling to stop from choking as Sabrina stared on with a glimmer in her eyes of pure happiness.

The hotel door behind her burst open.

***

In the Wynn Hotel on the Las Vegas Strip, Brodie's head hung over the toilet as he vomited his guts out in one of the restrooms on the casino-level floor. He held his stomach tightly as he stared into the bowl at what he had recently eaten. Glancing down, he saw his all-white shirt and pants were now covered in his vomit. His eyes rolled around in his head as he tried not to vomit anymore. He stared at some pills he had in his hand before throwing them in the toilet.

"I think Sabrina poisoned me. I got to call Cymone. We have to end this before someone dies," he said as his head fell off the toilet and hit the floor. "Sheila, I need your help, big sis." He looked up at the ceiling and then passed out on the floor.

***

Brodie reappeared in the time machine back at the Carmichael Science and Medical Institute. Sheila was right there. Like the times before, Brodie was in a coma-like state, which typically lasted around twenty-four to forty-eight hours. She checked his vitals.

"Your vitals are good. Let's just hope the 2030 Brodie is back."

Sheila looked at the note she had left herself on the wall. She saw the list of items to do. Terminate time machine two was scratched off the list.

"No more time travel from that room."

Sheila then looked at her phone and searched the internet for "March 12, 2015, *South Bend Tribune*." On the front page of the paper was her parent's house with the headline saying "Double Homicide Murder." As she read the article, she found out that KJ had been arrested for killing her parents. She then quickly turned her attention to their organizational chart to see if KJ was listed as an employee. She didn't see his name anywhere.

"Damn, what does that mean?"

She looked in her phone and saw Cymone's number. She quickly dialed it. Cymone answered.

"Hey, sis," Cymone said.

Sheila rejoiced. "I am so happy to hear your voice today."

"Is everything okay?" Cymone asked, curious about Sheila's reaction. "Where's Brodie?"

"It's going to be a late night," Sheila said. "I will bring him home to you, myself, tomorrow."

"Why are you going to do that?" Cymone asked.

"So, he can sleep in his own bed," Sheila replied a bit confused.

Cymone exhaled. "I guess Brodie didn't tell you yet that we are separated."

"Shit, no!" Sheila's mind raced trying to understand what could have happened for this to occur. "Why now?"

"I'm tired of waiting on him to stay at home more. I'm moving on with my life. He will always be the twins' father, but I need a life, too."

Sheila was at a loss for words. Cymone's doorbell rang.

"Girl, I have to go. That's Sabrina and her man. We're going on a double date. Please don't tell Brodie."

"Is the guy you're going out with named Derek?" Sheila asked as she thought about how all this change could have happened. *Sabrina and KJ from 2030 never returned, so this change can't be from them*, she thought.

"Yeah, it is. He's a businessman out of California. Seems like a great guy. Do you know him? Sabrina can't hold water."

"Sabrina didn't tell me."

"Then how did you find out his name?" Cymone asked thinking she was covering for Sabrina.

"I really don't know how. How did you meet this guy?"

"Through KJ, Sabrina's cousin. You know her cousin is like a multi-trillionaire or something ridiculous. I don't know how he does it, but he's never wrong about anything. It's like he already beat you guys in inventing a time machine, but he knows the future. I'm surprised Brodie didn't tell you about the hundred-billion-dollar deal KJ offered him for his technology. Of course, Brodie said no. For some reason, he hates KJ. I understand hating his uncle, but KJ didn't kill your parents."

"Damn, that's it! The older KJ, by staying in 2015, was able to help the younger KJ create wealth and power for himself," Sheila said to herself as she finally made sense of everything that must have happened. "He beat the system. They beat us."

"I do wish you would give Brodie another chance. He really loves you," Sheila said to Cymone.

"That's what Alaina and DeAndre said yesterday."

"Alaina and DeAndre are together?" Sheila asked, fuming.

"Why are you acting like this is new information? They have been married for five years now."

Sheila was almost in tears as she thought about how things had gotten out of their control. "I know things may be tough right now, but please don't give up on Brodie. He loves you."

"That window is closing. I still love him, but he has to be willing to change."

Sheila smirked as she glanced over at the time machine that Brodie had just come back in. "Yeah, I'm sure he will make the necessary changes." Suddenly, she stopped in her footsteps. A horrified look came to her face. "No," she said, shaking her head in disgust. "If there are two KJ's, then there's another Sabrina. Damn, they know the date that Brodie is coming back to!"

"Hey Sheila, I gotta go. Talk to you later," Cymone said trying to rush Sheila off the phone.

"Yeah, definitely," Sheila replied back frantically as she realized what the stakes were now that she figured out why things had changed so drastically. "Bye."

Cymone and Sheila hung up their phones.

Sheila quickly covered the window so that no one could look inside. She grabbed a piece of paper and wrote Brodie a note and placed it on the door so that he would hopefully read it before he exited out. She then grabbed her keys to enter the room and left them on the counter by the door. Before walking out the room, Sheila set the door to dead bolt lock from the inside in five seconds and she set her own personal code to prevent anyone from coming inside to bother Brodie beside herself. She also pressed the silent alarm on the wall to alert security of a security breach.

As Sheila walked out the room, Derek immediately covered her mouth and stuck a needle in her neck. As her body fell to the ground KJ and Sabrina stood over it. At the same time, Sabrina and

KJ heard the deadbolt lock activate. Sabrina tried her best to open the door, but couldn't.

"Now, how are we going to get inside the room?" Sabrina asked as she attempted to open the door again. "She's not waking up anytime soon now genius."

"Got to be a way inside," KJ said, trying to look through the window.

"With him inside with the only functional time machine, I'm sure he will travel back again, but this time he will go back further to end us for good."

"But if he comes out this door before going back it's over for him," KJ said gripping his gun. "He's not changing the life I've built."

"What are we going to do with her?"

KJ looked at Sabrina like she was stupid. "Like I know."

Sabrina searched Sheila's clothing for keys and any information she might have on her, but found nothing.

Sabrina and KJ both went over to the door control panel and tried to get in. Every code they input errored out.

"Damn, this bitch figured it out."

"Should we kill her?" KJ asked.

"Why? We need to keep her for leverage."

KJ went over to the door and started beating his fist on it in anger. After a while the note Sheila left for Brodie on the door fell down to the ground.

Two security guards came walking down the hallway, Sabrina dragged Sheila's body over behind the trashcan by the door away from their sightline. KJ started to reach for his gun, but stopped when he saw that the guards with their hands already on their guns. KJ and Sabrina stared at each other wondering what they were going to say as the guards got closer.

"Who are you two?" the tall black guard asked them. The smaller light skinned guard looked at KJ, Sabrina and the surroundings.

Sabrina smiled. "Hi, I'm Sabrina Simpson and this is my colleague KJ Wright. You've heard of Wright Enterprises, I know."

The two guards rolled their eyes.

"But what are you doing here?" the smaller guard asked, gripping his gun. "This is a restricted area."

"If you let me finish, I was going to tell you that we were meeting Mr. Carmichael and his sister to discuss business."

"How did you get in this section of the building without an escort?" the tall black guard asked.

"Another guard," KJ said with a smile hoping he was able to fool them.

"Wrong answer buddy," the smaller guard said, grabbing Sabrina while the other guard started to pull his gun out.

KJ rushed the guard before he was able to pull the gun out on them. They tussled and struggled for control of the gun as the other guard tried to help his partner. Sabrina grabbed the smaller guard's gun and shot it up into the ceiling. She held one gun on the smaller guard while now the taller guard held his gun on KJ.

"Just let him go and we will leave the premises," she said, cocking the gun back.

From the floor, the taller guard saw Sheila's feet. KJ saw what the guard noticed.

"She's not dead," KJ said.

"Nobody has to die today as long as we walk out this building," Sabrina said. "Let him come to me."

"I can't do that," the taller guard said, looking in his partner's sorrowful eyes.

Sabrina saw that the guard was not going to let KJ go. She felt like she was out of options especially since surrendering wasn't an option. Sabrina looked KJ in the eyes as if to signal him. Without a notice, she shot the officer in the head. KJ quickly fell to his left. As he hit the floor, the taller officer shot him twice, once in the right leg and the other in his side, before Sabrina shot the guard several times in the chest. KJ bled everywhere as Sabrina came to assist him.

"We got to get out of here. You need a hospital."

"What about Sheila?" KJ asked.

"Fuck that bitch. Fuck Brodie too. KJ, it isn't worth it. We got everything we ever wanted. Losing your life isn't worth it."

KJ saw her point. She grabbed the small guard's access badge and they went out the back stairwell and then down the back entrance to their car. KJ was unconscious when she opened the back door to the car and put him inside. Sabrina quickly raced off toward the hospital. As she drove down the street, a parade of police cars raced toward the building.

When the police got inside the building, they saw the two dead guards and Sheila laying there still unconscious. The paramedics looked at her and could tell that she was drugged by her dilated pupils. They rushed her off to the hospital.

Chapter Sixteen

It had been twenty-four hours after the incident that led to the two officers' deaths, when Brodie came to his senses. He woke up disoriented and thirsty. On the table next to the bed was a case of bottled water. He drank about four sixteen-ounce water bottles in a row without stopping. As he got out of the chair, he fumbled around the room. It was odd to him that Sheila was nowhere to be found. Typically, Sheila was the first face he saw and she made things easier to adjust back to normal while he recovered. Even without her presence, Brodie knew Sheila must have left a note of some kind since she wasn't there. But with all his fumbling around the office, he actually pushed the note that fell on the ground even further under the steel metal file cabinet by the door. Still unsure and very suspicious, Brodie was hesitant to leave the room. He noticed that the see-through window on the door was covered up. He peeked outside and saw nothing until he took a closer look and saw smeared blood on the walls. He closed it. Brodie paranoia increased. His eyes surveyed the office until it saw the cell phone in the wall cabinet with glass windows. He grabbed it and called Sheila, but got no answer. He then called Cymone.

"Hello," Cymone answered, somewhat irritated. "Brodie, where have you been?"

"I'm working, but will be home soon."

"Maybe you need to see a doctor. Brodie, this isn't your home anymore. We agreed that you would move out three months ago.

I can't go backwards with you anymore. This is proof that you can't change."

Brodie was speechless on the other end of the phone. He didn't understand what could have happened. Then it struck him like lightning. He thought back to his time travel and that the present day KJ had never returned since Sheila probably shut down the other time machine. He grimaced when it hit him that with the present day KJ stuck in the past that also meant that he had knowledge of the future and could change everything that he had went back to correct.

"Damn," Brodie said going over to the chair to sit down. Just the thought of the damage that KJ might have caused was overbearing to him.

"Who you saying damn to?" Cymone replied back with attitude.

"Not you. Sorry. Have you seen my sister Sheila?"

"No, we spoke yesterday. You need to tell her what happened between us. She thought you still lived here. I don't want this divorce to be messy on the kids."

"Divorce? Kids? What did I do Cymone?"

"Really? You gonna play dumb?" She smirked. "Brodie, I don't have time to rehash the same old story again and again."

"I want to make things better. You're the only woman for me. I love you more than life," Brodie pleaded.

"Brodie, I didn't want to tell you like this, but I have started dating someone. And he has time for me."

"What the hell? We're not even divorced yet and you are already on the market?" he asked, getting even more frustrated.

"Someone else shows interest in me and now you want to be my husband. This has been our relationship for far too long. I have accepted your absence and missing our kid's events at school, but no more. You are on your own."

"What are you talking about?" Brodie asked.

"On the phone like we're some long-distance relationship. I'm tired of the lonely nights while you sleep in your lab. I needed you here. The kids needed you here."

"But I have provided for my family," Brodie said.

Cymone chuckled. "Money isn't everything. You have missed teacher conferences, music recitals, soccer games and the list goes on. You don't even know how your kids are doing at school."

"I…" he started to say, but she cut him off.

"Don't know!" Cymone said rolling her eyes as if he could see her through the phone.

"Who are you dating?" Brodie asked, changing the subject.

"Just a guy that Sabrina introduced to me."

"Sabrina! Why are you hanging out with her? She can't be trusted."

"Trust? You are so full of yourself. If you're worried about Sabrina being trusted then you should tell your brother since that's his wife's best friend."

"His wife?"

"Your brother is married to Alaina."

"He married Alaina?" Brodie repeated.

Cymone huffed. She felt Brodie was mocking her. "I don't have time for these games."

"I love you, Cymone. Please believe that."

In the background, Brodie heard Cymone's doorbell and the door open. He then heard a male voice say, "I brought you back some coffee. Thanks for last night."

"Cymone," Brodie yelled through the phone. "Are my kids there?"

"No, they are not. Bye Brodie," Cymone said as she hung up the phone on him.

Brodie collapsed to the floor feeling hopeless. The thought of Cymone being with another man broke his heart. While on the floor, he tried to think of ways to correct everything that had now transpired in the new present. Going back into the time machine seemed to be the only option to get Cymone back, stop KJ, and to make sure Sheila was safe. The problem was that Sheila was the only person he trusted to make sure he returned on time and recovered. With her whereabouts unknown he didn't want to take the risk of being stuck in the past.

"I got to find Sheila."

At the hospital, sleeping in the bed was Sheila. Her stomach had been pumped and she had been given medicine to counteract the drug that KJ had given her the night before, but she was still unconscious. The nurse called Brodie since he was first on her contact list.

"Hello," Brodie asked. He was still in the office contemplating his next move.

"Hi, I'm nurse Connie. I'm calling from Memorial Hospital. Are you Brodie Carmichael, Sheila Carmichael's brother?"

"Yes, that me. Is she okay?"

"Your sister was admitted last night. We tried to reach you, but no one answered. She had some procedures last night, but is resting now."

"What happened to her?"

"You will need to speak to the police about that matter."

"Okay, I'll be up there soon," Brodie said, hanging up the phone.

Brodie looked around the office and grabbed the door knob. He was fearful of what might be on the other side of the door, but he knew in order to go back in time and change the future that KJ created he needed Sheila's help to do it.

Brodie slowly unlocked the door and exited out. The hallway was empty except for some yellow police tape down the other hallway, which wasn't seen from the office window. His fear increased. Brodie made sure he had his car keys and bolted out of the building. He used the car keys to find the car by constantly hitting the unlock button. Once he heard the beep, he jumped in his car and sped off.

At the hospital, Brodie ran in. As he was going to the nurse station, he saw Sabrina in the waiting room, but she didn't see him. He didn't understand why she was there. Brodie went to Sheila's room and sat down next to her bed. He grabbed her hand.

"Sheila, this is all my fault. I'm so sorry, sis. I screwed up."

Sheila slowly opened her eyes and looked at him. "Yes, you did."

He smiled at her. "KJ and Sabrina really set this all up."

"They beat us," she mumbled as she tried to clear her dry mouth.

Brodie passed her the cup of water that was on the side of the bed. She drank it and held out the cup for more. She drank that too.

"Yeah, I don't know what to do now," he said staring at her.

"Brodie, there's only one thing we can and you know what that is."

Brodie dropped his head. "I don't want to do that."

Sheila sat up a little bit on the bed. "This isn't about Cymone anymore. You didn't lose her because KJ and Sabrina. You lost her because of you."

Brodie nodded his head agreeing with her. "Maybe KJ can change."

Sheila rolled her eyes. "I'm here because of them. He stuck a needle in my neck. I don't think he's changing at all. It's either we die or they die."

"I can't do it," Brodie said.

"You don't have a choice, little brother."

"If you are in the hospital, I can't go by myself. What if I get stuck back there?"

Sheila exhaled. "It worked out for KJ getting stuck back there. But I'll be there to make sure you make it back."

In the doorway behind Brodie came Detective Johnson, an old white man with a southern accent.

"Excuse me," Sheila said, noticing the detective at the door.

Detective Johnson stepped inside the room and walked to the foot of the bed.

"I take it that you are Brodie Carmichael, her brother, and the head of the Carmichael Center." He stared at Brodie like he was guilty of something.

"Yes, that's me."

"Where were you last night when this happened? And don't say at home with your wife that would be very disappointing to hear since I just got off the phone with her and she stated that she was on a date last night. Ouch!"

Brodie fumed. "I was at my sister's house sleeping."

"And it took this long for you to come check on your sister?"

"Are you trying to accuse me of hurting my own sister?" Brodie asked, staring him down into the ground.

"It's not just about your sister buddy. Two of your security guards were gunned down as well."

Brodie felt bad. "Hey, I didn't know that happened. I got to contact their families."

"And now you care?" Detective Johnson said with a smirk.

"Are you even being serious right now?" Sheila asked. "My brother was at my house. He wouldn't do this to me or kill anybody in a trillion years, officer. Look at the security footage, I'm sure you will see who did this."

"The videotapes were erased." Detective Johnson leered over at Brodie. "I wonder who has access to that?"

"It wasn't my brother who did this."

"How do you know?" Detective Johnson asked.

"I know. Just leave us alone, please," Sheila said, turning away from the detective.

The detective saw that Sheila and Brodie were done talking to him. "Just don't leave town," he said as he walked out the door.

"What a joke?" Brodie said. "He wanted to blame me for this. That's crazy."

"You know the police is always trying to make their work quick and easy."

Brodie got a bright idea. "Oh snap, I think I figured it out."

"What?" Sheila saw how excited he was and wanted to know why.

Brodie looked at her and then stopped all emotion. "I can't tell you."

"What do you mean you can't tell me?" Sheila asked with an attitude.

"Just bear with me, sis. I don't want to spoil anything that may or may not come true. Are you okay to get out of here?"

Sheila sat up on the bed some more. "Is that officer lurking in the hallway?"

Brodie got up and looked out the door. He didn't see anyone. "The coast is clear. Are you sure you're ready?"

"Yeah, I just want to get back to the life we know and should have."

"Me too."

Brodie helped Sheila get out of the bed. She put on the clothes she wore to the hospital which Brodie found in the closet. They slowly walked to the stairwell and went down the stairs to the parking garage. Brodie had her wait by the door as he went to get his car. He picked her up and they drove out the parking garage. When they passed by the front of the hospital, Brodie and Sabrina locked eyes. She took off for her car.

"Why is Sabrina here?" Sheila asked.

"I think there was a shootout. I'm thinking KJ got shot. Sabrina must have killed both of the guards."

"Did KJ die?" Sheila asked.

"I don't know and we don't have time to figure it out. I'm sure Sabrina is coming for us. She loves her cousin deeply."

At the lab, Sheila locked the doors behind as Brodie got into the time machine.

"This time I'm going to get it right," he said.

"I already set the time back to when KJ was like eighteen. He said he used to drink a lot in high school. Make it look like a car accident," Sheila said expressing the importance of KJ dying.

When Sheila turned her back, Brodie changed the time back to the time he went back last time, March 11, 2015 at Central State University. It wasn't until he disappeared that Sheila noticed that he had changed the time.

"Damn you, Brodie," she said knowing what he was attempting to do. "You only have four hours this time."

Brodie appeared out of thin air on the campus of Central State University. He quickly looked at his watch and saw that the date was March 11, 2015, and the time was 5:30 p.m.

"Sorry, Sheila." He saw the younger version of himself strolling along right past him without even noticing that he was there. "You were so dumb. Wake up man."

Out of nowhere, he saw KJ appear on the other side of the yard like before.

KJ saw him and then looked at the younger Brodie. He pulled out a gun and started to walk toward the younger Brodie. Older Brodie ran down the younger Brodie and grabbed him, and the younger Brodie finally saw the resemblance.

"Do I know you?" the younger Brodie asked with his fist up.

"That guy over there is about to kill you. We need to get you to a safe place."

"Who?" the younger Brodie asked. Then he looked over and saw KJ running towards them with his gun in hand. This time around KJ started shooting at them.

"What is going on?" the younger Brodie asked hysterically as the campus went into a frenzy with students running for their lives.

"Come with me," Older Brodie said as they ran across the street. Like before, he noticed a college student at the credit union getting cash out of the ATM who had left his car running. They ran to it and jumped in.

"What is this about?" the Young Brodie asked.

"You wouldn't believe me if I told you," Older Brodie said.

"Well, I'm getting out." Young Brodie got out of the car as it started moving.

Older Brodie noticed Older KJ looking for them. He stopped the car, jumped out, and punched his younger self and then threw him in the trunk. "You'll thank me later."

He jumped back in the car and drove off. As he passed through a stop light, older KJ saw him.

Brodie made it back home in South Bend, Indiana in about two hours flat. When he walked in his house his parents like before were watching Jeopardy.

"What are you doing here, Brodie?" his mother asked, while his father gave him the side-eye. "You look older. Are you stressed at school like that?"

"Mom, I'm not stressed out. I'm healthy and fine," Brodie said with a smile.

His mother and father looked at each other curious about his new appearance.

"Daddy, I came home because somebody told me that Sheila was in trouble and some people wanted to hurt her."

"What do you mean by hurt her?" his father asked as he sat up on the couch. "I'm getting my gun." His father got up and went to his bedroom.

Gloria got up from the couch and looked him in the eye. "Are you really serious, Brodie?"

"Momma, I'm not playing around with you. You need to go the basement and wait until all this is over." He looked at his watch. He noticed the time left being fifty minutes. "What the hell?"

His father returned with two guns in his hands. "Are these people coming over here?"

"That's what I heard. I just don't want nothing to happen to you guys."

His father held up the guns. "Nothing happening to me. I'm going to sit right here in the dark and wait for them to come in this house. Bang!"

"I'll go get Sheila from the corner store," Brodie said.

"How do you know she went there?" Gloria asked.

"Call it intuition," Brodie said with a smirk. "Please, go to the basement momma."

His mother went toward the basement door. She kept looking at Brodie wondering what was really going on. After a few minutes by the door, she went down into the basement.

Brodie ran down the street to the corner store. When he got inside, he saw his sister in the dairy section. Like before, he scoped the store to see if anybody was there aside from him, her, and the store clerk. He saw no one. He slowly walked over to his sister.

"Sheila," he said from behind her.

She turned around and jumped. Everything that she had in her hands fell to the floor. "Shoot! Brodie, what are you doing here?" She grabbed her mouth to hold back from screaming. Her eyes bulged out in amazement.

"I…"

Sheila yelled. She couldn't control herself. "It worked. Oh my God, it actually worked. Damn, you look older."

"You know?" Brodie asked, wondering what she was talking about.

"I never believed that time travel would be taken seriously. People always laughed at me. What year are you from?"

"2030."

"Fifteen years from now. You look pretty good for your age, bro. What about me? Am I married? Do I have kids? So many questions I have."

"I can't tell you," he said, slightly looking away. "But we need to hurry. I only have." He looked at his watch. "Forty minutes now."

She could tell something was wrong. "Why are you here?"

Brodie sighed. "I came to save you."

"From what?"

"KJ is coming to kill all of us."

Sheila laughed loudly. "You got to be joking. I just met KJ. He seems like cool people, not a killer. He's meeting me here in a few minutes." She paused and then realized what was happening. "He killed me already?"

"That's how they know where you are each time."

"I'm dead in the future?" Sheila asked upset.

Brodie nodded. "I came back to save you, Mom, and Dad. The KJ from my time wants us dead. He came here before and is stuck in the time continuum. He made his younger self the richest man in the world by using this time machine."

Sheila exhaled. "Where have you been so far? Have you seen the 2030 KJ here?"

"Yeah, he was chasing me and my younger self around Central State's campus."

"Where is the younger you at now?" Sheila asked with a concerned look on her face.

"He's safe. I locked him up in my trunk. KJ needs me dead more than anything. I figure he's on his way here to find me and probably kill us all."

"What are we doing? We have to kill KJ."

Brodie let out a light chuckle. "Damn, you are consistent on the death of KJ."

"So, I am alive in 2030?" she asked with a smile on her face.

"I'll tell you everything on the way back home."

"Shouldn't we go as far away as possible?" Sheila asked confused why they would go to where KJ expected them to be.

"Not this time around."

"Let's go," Sheila said, as she headed to the store's exit.

They jumped in her car and took off. As they were making a right turn, 2030 KJ was parking his car in front of the store.

***

About twenty-five minutes later, KJ walked into their house quiet as a mouse. He was ready to shoot upon seeing any movement. As he walked in the living room, Brodie and his father, Paul, waited on the couch. It was so dark that KJ couldn't see anything in the room. He searched for a light switch on the wall. As he found it and clicked on, Brodie's father, Paul, shot him in the chest, killing him instantly.

"Is that him?" his father asked.

Brodie went over and looked at KJ's face. "Yeah, that's him."

As Brodie called the police, his mother, Gloria, and Sheila came up from the basement. Sheila went to Brodie.

"How much time now?" she asked.

Brodie looked at his watch. "Thirty seconds."

"I love you Brodie."

"Just make sure to get me out of the trunk."

"They weren't supposed to live, were they?" Sheila asked with a smile looking at their parents.

"See you soon, sis. Make sure to avoid being close to KJ and Sabrina," Brodie said as he slowly disappeared. "Check to make sure this KJ didn't contact the young KJ." The second sentence about the KJ's connection was filled with static so it was hard for Sheila to understand what he wanted her to do.

"What did he say?" she asked herself looking at the spot that he vanished from.

***

Brodie reappeared in the room he had left before. After a day of recuperating, he was back to normal. He grabbed the note of instructions he had left for himself to follow on the wall. He read them over. Sheila was the first person he saw as she walked in smiling. He was happy to see his big sister.

"Hey, is mom and dad living?

She looked at him like he was crazy. "No. They both died from Coronavirus in 2020."

Brodie got emotional thinking about their death. "I did everything possible and they didn't make it."

Sheila put her hand on his shoulder to comfort him. "Brodie, even the best laid plans can't predict a dangerous virus from popping up during time travel. A lot can happen over fifteen years."

"Man. Maybe I should go back."

"I don't want to hear this today. I'm tired. And the last thing I want is to relive them dying again. Somethings you can't change."

"Is Cymone alive?" he asked afraid of the answer.

"Yeah. I called her a few minutes ago and told her you would be home soon. She and the kids were happy to hear it."

"So, me and her are good."

"Definitely. That woman loves you to death." Sheila smiled. "Hell, my kids are excited to see you too."

Brodie froze. "You have kids?"

"Yes dummy."

"By who?"

"Derek, jokester." Sheila showed him her wedding ring.

"Damn," he said under his breath.

"Are you okay?" Sheila saw the ill look on his face.

"Did you shut down the other time machine?" Brodie asked, looking in her happy face.

"I did, but after talking with Derek he thinks it's a bad idea. KJ thinks it's bad too."

"Are they both in the building right now?" Brodie asked nervously.

"By the way, what did you say to me in the past before you left?"

Brodie turned to look at her. "I told you to make sure the KJ's didn't connect. I think they did."

"Why do you think that?"

"You're married to Derek. That's why."

"Well, we do own half the company."

"Shit! This is their plan, sis. This isn't love. The Older KJ connected and gave him instructions to follow. If they get to that other time machine, we're all toast."

"I don't believe you. I would think that you would want me happy. I don't say anything about you being with Cymone."

"This is different," Brodie said with anger, frustrated that his sister didn't understand.

"That's my family Brodie," Sheila said, staring him down.

Cymone walked into the room. Their eyes met. Brodie smiled as tears came to his eyes. Cymone approached him looking beautiful and elegant.

"I love you baby," Brodie said as he kissed her.

"Are you going back in that time travel machine?" she asked.

Brodie looked at her and thought about things that he still wanted to change, but seeing her and seeing the love in her eyes made him know that he didn't want to change the love he felt for her or that she felt for him. He embraced her.

"I think it's time we end time travel for good."

Cymone kissed him. "That is the best thing I've heard in years."

Derek and KJ came into the room.

"I know it's early, but we want to use the other time machine next week," KJ asked.

"Why?" Brodie asked back.

"A history fact finding trip," Derek said looking over at Sheila for her to help in the discussion.

"Yeah, Brodie, we just think we can use time travel to see what really happened in the past. Not to change the past."

Cymone looked at Brodie. She could tell it wasn't something he wanted to do.

"Sure," Brodie said with a smile. Everyone in the room was shocked by his response.

Sheila stared at him. "Are you okay?"

"Sis, I couldn't be better. Let's go out to eat tonight."

Everyone in the room was cool with the dinner suggestion.

"I need to change and fix my hair," Sheila said looking at the mirror on the wall. "Let's go home. Me and Derek will meet you guys around six at the Emporium."

"Sounds great," Cymone said. "Are you coming, KJ?"

KJ smiled. He stared at Brodie still confused by his quick agreement on them going into the time machine. "Definitely. I love to eat."

"Great," Brodie said.

KJ, Derek, and Sheila all left the room. Cymone snuggled up on the bed with Brodie. After about ten minutes, Brodie woke her up.

"Go to security to make sure that they all left," Brodie said.

"What's going on?" Cymone asked, a bit confused by his abrupt demeanor.

"Just do this for me, please."

Cymone left the room as Brodie got up and put on some clothes. Cymone quickly came back.

"They all left."

"Great."

Brodie went to time machine number one and took out the programming chips. He put them in his back pocket. He went to time machine number two and took out the programming chips too. But this time he smashed the chips and crushed the motherboard so that it would never be used again.

Cymone rushed to him, thinking he had lost his mind. "Why did you do that?"

Brodie stared into her eyes. "Derek and KJ are lying."

"How do you know?" Cymone asked.

"This isn't my first rodeo with them two. I can't let them change the past again."

"What do you mean by again?" Cymone was curious. "This wasn't the first time?"

"No."

Cymone was in shock. "What happened before?"

"You were with Derek."

"Oh no," Cymone said as she grabbed the hammer and hit the motherboard again. "I get it now. I don't want to change being with you."

"You are all that I have ever wanted. Are you sure you don't want to go back again?"

"The past is the past and it shouldn't be altered for any reason. Life should have its limitations."

They kissed as Brodie grabbed her hand and they walked out the room. As Brodie and Cymone got in the car, KJ was back in the building frantically running down the hallway towards the time machine lab rooms. When he saw the destruction of the control panels, he dropped to his knees in anger.

"I knew it! I knew it! I'm going to get you one day, Brodie. That's a promise."

CPSIA information can be obtained
at www.ICGtesting.com
Printed in the USA
LVHW052016230621
690962LV00015B/714